Want to get closer to the Doctor
and learn more about the very best
Doctor Who books out there?

Go to
www.doctorwhochildrensbooks.co.uk
for news, reviews, competitions
and more!

BBC Children's Books

Published by the Penguin Group

Penguin Books Ltd, 80 Strand, London, WC2R 0RL, England

Penguin Group (USA) Inc., 375 Hudson Street, New York 10014, USA

Penguin Books (Australia) Ltd, 250 Camberwell Road, Camberwell,

Victoria 3124, Australia (A division of Pearson Australia Group PTY Ltd)

Penguin Group (NZ), 67 Apollo Drive, Rosedale, North Shore

0632, New Zealand (A division of Pearson New Zealand Ltd)

Canada, India, South Africa

Published by BBC Children's Books, 2012

Text and design © Children's Character Books

Terrible Lizards by Jonanthan Green

Horror of the Space Snakes by Gary Russell

Cover illustrations by Kev Walker and Paul Campbell

001 – 10 9 8 7 6 5 4 3 2 1

ISBN – 978-14059-0-804-7

Mixed Sources
Product group from well-managed
forests and other controlled sources
www.fsc.org Cert no. SA-COC-1592
© 1996 Forest Stewardship Council
FSC

Printed in Great Britain by Clays Ltd, St Ives plc

CONTENTS

TERRIBLE LIZARDS 11

1. YOU DON'T WANT TO GO TO MARS 13

2 CHANCE OF RAIN LATER 19

3. STOWAWAYS 25

4. A LONG WAY FROM HOME 30

5. THAR SHE BLOWS! 36

6. LEVIATHAN 43

7. ISHMAEL 50

8. WELCOME TO FLORIDA 54

9. READY WHEN YOU ARE 62

10. UPSTREAM 66

11. OCCUPATIONAL HAZARD 71

12. TERRIBLE LIZARD 77

13. CARNIVORE 84

14. GERONIMO! 93

15. WHAT HAPPENED TO THE SKY? 97

16. HERE BE DRAGONS 103

17. MR AND MRS POND 109

18. JUST ADD WATER 115

19. FLOTSAM AND JETSAM 121

20. TOO CLOSE FOR COMFORT 127

21. THE BIGGER PICTURE 133

22. ONE IN A TRILLION 138

23. ON WINGS OF FIRE 144

24. ZOMBIE DINOSAURS 151

25. A MILLION TIMES WORSE 157

26. NO MORE TO LOSE 162

27. ALL GOOD THINGS............................. 165

28. BUKET OF BOLTS............................ 172

29. DAMAGE LIMITATION............................ 178

30. A SECOND CHANCE............................ 182

31. LIFE'S LITTLE MYSTERIES 187

HORROR OF THE SPACE SNAKES 193

1. TRAVELLING MAN 195

2. NEW SUNSHINE MORNING................................210

3. LIFE IN A DAY 220

4. GREAT LEAP FORWARD................................226

5. CYNICAL HEART 236

6. I TRAVEL 246

7. LET THE CHILDREN SPEAK................................264

8. SPACEFACE................................285

9. SEE THE LIGHTS................................295

10. REPULSION 304

11. MONSTER................................315

12. HUNTER AND THE HUNTED................................321

13. BULLETPROOF HEART................................336

14. BANGING ON THE DOOR................................352

15. STARS WILL LEAD THE WAY................................359

16. ALIVE AND KICKING................................375

DOCTOR WHO

TERRIBLE LIZARDS

JONATHAN GREEN

CHAPTER ONE
YOU DON'T WANT TO GO TO MARS

'So, who do you want to see first?' the Doctor asked. He flicked the floppy fringe of dark hair out of his eyes with a jerk of his head and fixed Amy with an intense stare.

She stared back.

He might look like a young man but he had the oldest eyes in the universe. And he dressed like a geography teacher.

'Who have we got?'

'How about Michelangelo painting the ceiling of the Sistine Chapel?' the Doctor suggested.

He danced around the TARDIS's hexagonal control console, pulling a lever here and cranking a handle there. 'Or Caravaggio? Or Leonardo Da Vinci painting the Mona Lisa? Although I've met him before, so we'd have to time our visit quite carefully. But of course, it's up to you. So what's it to be? The Renaissance awaits!'

'Oh, it's so hard to decide,' Amy squealed in delight. 'It's just so exciting. First I get to meet Vincent van Gogh and now the Renaissance!'

'I was quite keen on visiting Olympus Mons on Mars,' said the young man leaning against the balcony railing. He clearly wasn't expecting good weather in the Late Middle Ages as he was already wearing his winter vest. 'Did you know that it's the largest volcano in the Solar System?'

'In your solar system perhaps,' the Doctor muttered.

Rory looked at him, a hurt expression on his face.

'Oh, come on Rory!' the Doctor laughed. 'You don't want to go to Mars. It's just... red. Very red.

Red everywhere in fact.'

'And what's wrong with red?' Amy asked, peering at the Doctor from behind a tress of auburn hair.

'Nothing,' the Doctor backtracked quickly. 'Nothing at all. Lots of great things are red. Strawberries for instance. Strawberries are great. I love strawberries. And sunsets. Very lovely things, sunsets. It's just that Mars is a bit... boring. Well, dangerous. Actually more like lethal. You might as well say you want to stop by a Welsh quarry, or a mining village for that matter.'

The Doctor, Amy and Rory shot each other several anxious glances.

'Yes,' the Doctor went on, 'let's not go there again. Not after what happened the last time.'

'Oh, come on, Doctor, I'm only kidding with you.' Now it was Amy's turn to laugh. 'Besides,' she said, grabbing Rory by the arm and giving it a squeeze, 'a bit of culture will be good for you, Mr Pond.'

'Alright,' Rory said, 'just so long as we steer clear of Venice this time.'

The Doctor and Amy looked at each other again.

'Good point, well made,' the Doctor said and flicked a switch on the TARDIS console.

A resounding crash shook the control room. Amy felt the floor give way beneath her and suddenly she and Rory were falling. They collided with the railing surrounding the console platform and grabbed hold, both winded and shaken.

The Doctor was still clinging onto the control console itself, looking down at them across the sloping floor with a startled expression on his face.

'Was that you?' Amy asked.

'No! Of course not,' the Doctor replied.

'Only remember you've been flying this thing with the brakes on for the last nine hundred years!'

'It's closer to eight hundred actually, but never mind that now.'

'So, if it wasn't you, Doctor,' Rory cut in, 'what was it?'

Suddenly the TARDIS lurched again and the three companions found themselves stumbling back across the platform the other way.

'Whoa there!' the Doctor yelled, only just managing to keep a hold of the control console as Amy and Rory crashed into the barrier on the other side. 'I think we just collided with something.'

'I know I did,' Rory gasped, clutching his side.

'While travelling through time?' Amy screwed up her face in annoyance. 'Now why doesn't that surprise me, Doctor? Does that sort of thing happen a lot?'

'No,' the Doctor replied. 'Not that often anyway.'

The eerie tolling of the Cloister Bell echoed from the juddering walls of the control chamber.

'Uh-oh,' Amy said quietly. She shot the Doctor a look of wild alarm.

'Uh-oh?' Rory said. 'I don't like the sound of that.'

The Time Lord looked at them. 'Neither do I.'

'So what does it mean?' Amy asked.

'I'd hold onto something if I were you,' the Doctor said, doing another manic circuit of the control console.

'Why?' asked Rory.

'Because I think it means we're going to crash.'

CHAPTER TWO
CHANCE OF RAIN LATER

The asthmatic wheezing of the TARDIS's engines filled the room as the Doctor's blue box tumbled through the Vortex.

'We need to land the old girl and fast!' the Doctor announced. He grabbed hold of a handle that looked like it should belong to an old-fashioned record player and started winding it rapidly.

'What do you want us to do?' Amy shouted over the howling of the engines as she managed to grab hold of the console. The doom-laden ringing of the bell continued to echo around the chamber.

'Pond, keep that crank next to your right hand steady!'

'This one?' she said, grabbing hold of a lever. The chamber listed again, pitching them all sideways.

'No!' the Doctor cried out in alarm. 'The red one!'

'Then why didn't you say the red one in the first place?' Amy protested, correcting her mistake. 'Ugh! Men!'

'What about me? Is there anything I can do?' Rory asked.

'The blue stabilisers!' the Doctor shouted over the dreadful wailing of the crashing TARDIS. 'Keep your hands on the blue stabilisers!'

Rory did as he was told.

'Now what?' Amy asked, as the three of them hung on against the whirling motion of the TARDIS.

The Doctor watched the rise and fall of the time rotor for a moment before answering. His face was bathed in the eerie greeny-orange glow of the control room lights, making him look like some weird alien goblin.

'Now hang on!' the Doctor yelled, an expression of boyish delight on his face, and flicked another switch. 'Geronimo!'

The TARDIS continued to shake as it spun faster and faster, whirling through the temporal turmoil of the Vortex. And then suddenly it stopped.

Rory slipped from where he had been clinging onto the control console and landed with a thud on the platform floor. 'Ow,' he said.

'Where are we?' Amy asked, leaving Rory to pick himself up off the floor.

'Earth,' the Doctor replied. Pulling a monitor down from the above the console he took a closer look, his eyebrows knitting together as he did so.

'Can you be a little more precise than that?' Amy asked.

'Hmm?' The Doctor turned his attention from the monitor to his companion. 'Oh, I see what you mean.' He glanced at the monitor again. 'Oh, you know, the usual. Nitrogen roughly seventy-eight per cent. Oxygen twenty per cent. Sunny, with a slight chance of rain later. A little less pollution than you're used to but a bit of fresh air never hurt anyone now, did it?'

'Great,' Amy said, taking Rory by the hand and making for the door, 'let's take a look outside then!'

'Righty-ho, you do that,' the Doctor called back, still distracted. 'Just don't... break anything.'

'We'll try not to,' Amy laughed. She paused at the door, Rory stumbling to a halt behind her. 'Are you not coming?'

'No, not just yet. You kids go on ahead,' the Doctor replied. 'I just want to make sure the old girl's okay. I mean we don't want her blowing up... again... or anything. Besides, the TARDIS appears to have detected an anomalous temporal signature and I want to double-check the readings. You know, make sure it's not a phase echo from the collision or anything like that.'

'What?' Amy grunted.

The Doctor thought for a moment. 'Wibbly-wobbly, timey-wimey stuff,' he said at last.

'Okey-dokey. But don't be too long.' Amy

opened the door. 'You don't want to miss out on all the fun, do you?'

And with that she stepped through.

'Oh.'

'What is it?' Rory started. 'Hey! The ground's moving.'

'That's because we're not on the ground,' Amy said, looking around her, eyes wide with surprise.

Rory did the same. 'Oh,' he said quietly.

The creak of cables and the groaning of steel filled the air around them. A stinging, sea salt breeze buffeted their faces and ran airy fingers through their hair. The deck rolled beneath their feet.

'We're on a ship.'

'I know,' said Amy.

'At sea.'

'I know. And we're not alone.'

Amy returned the stare of the grizzled, weather-beaten face in front of her, before taking in the rest of the circle of rough-looking men surrounding them. They were a mix of nationalities and their clothes looked strangely dated.

The sailors scowled back at them.

Rory swallowed hard. 'But they're...' His voice trailed off.

Amy looked from the men to her husband and back again.

'I know,' she gasped. 'Pirates!'

Rory gave a weary sigh. 'Again?'

CHAPTER THREE
STOWAWAYS

'Doctor!' Amy called back through the TARDIS door. 'I think you should come out now.'

'Yes,' the Doctor replied. His attention was fixed on the monitor in front of him. 'Just give me a minute longer, can you?'

He spun a wheel beside him. An image began to form on the screen. He gasped. 'The crack in Amelia's wall.'

He twiddled a knob on the side of the monitor, bringing the image into sharp focus.

'No, not the crack in Amelia's wall! But a fracture nonetheless. A fracture in time. Several in fact, and close together.'

'Doctor!' Amy called again. 'We could really do with your help out here.'

'Yes, yes. All right, I'm coming,' he fussed.

Rummaging in a pocket of his tweed jacket, he pulled out a crumpled raffle ticket and a stub of pencil. He smoothed out the ticket and scribbled down a set of coordinates, before returning both pencil and paper to his pocket.

The Doctor leapt down the steps from the control console platform. He skidded across the floor and threw himself through the door.

'Now, what seems to be the problem?' He said, blinking in the early morning sunlight that greeted him.

His arrival was accompanied by the clatter of weapons being readied and pointed in his direction.

'Ah,' he said, taking in the sailors and the assortment of pistols and knives they were holding in their hands.

Amy, Rory and the Doctor were completely surrounded.

'You must be the welcoming committee.'

'And you're coming with us,' a large man said in a voice that rumbled like pebbles being tossed on a beach. His skin was the colour of polished ebony, he was wearing a Bosun's cap, and he had a gun in his hand.

'Right you are then,' the Doctor said.

He took a step forwards, quickly scanning the rolling deck of the ship, taking in the large black funnel and the lifeboats secured to the gunwales. There was the tarry smell of coal in the air. The TARDIS had materialized at the bow of the tramp steamer, below the bridge.

'It's this way is it?' he said, jerking a thumb to his left.

The large Nigerian said nothing. He simply gestured with his pistol that the Doctor and his companions should get moving.

The rest of the ship's crew continued to stare at the three time travellers as they were forced to move away from the safety of the TARDIS.

'Back to work, the lot of you!' the bosun shouted. The crowd dispersed as the large man marched his captives up a staircase of rusted iron to the deck above.

Amy and Rory were forced to grab onto the railings as the ship continued to heave under them. The Doctor bounded up the steps quite happily without having to hold onto anything.

At the top of the steps the bosun pointed them towards a rattling wooden door. Passing through it they entered the bridge of the steam ship. Amy took in the cabin at a glance. There wasn't a single piece of electronic equipment visible anywhere. It was all glass-fronted dials and gauges, and finely worked metal.

There were two men already inside the cabin. They were poring over the age-worn maps and crinkled sea charts spread out on a table between them. The closest was wearing a white peaked cap, underneath which his hair was grey and close-cropped, like his beard. The other, on the far side of the table, was taller and younger. A luxurious black moustache adorned his top lip. He was dressed in a smart, pale linen jacket and plus fours.

Neither man looked up as the Doctor, Rory and Amy were herded into the cramped cabin.

The bosun cleared his throat loudly.

'What is it, Mr Hayes?' the older man said, still studying the maps in front of him.

'Stowaways, Captain,' the dark-skinned Mr Hayes replied. 'We found these three down below.'

It was only then that the two men even bothered to look up. They took in the Doctor, Amy and Rory with disdainful glances.

'Captain! A pleasure to meet you,' the Doctor said. He thrust his hand out towards the older man.

'Just who might you be?' the Captain growled. 'And what are you doing on my ship?'

The Time Lord withdrew his hand and straightened his bow tie instead. The two men were glowering at him now. He beamed back at them, a mischievous sparkle in his eye.

'It's all right,' he said, 'you can trust me. I'm the Doctor.'

CHAPTER FOUR
A LONG WAY FROM HOME

The Captain arched his eyebrows. 'Is that supposed to mean something to me?' he said.

'No, obviously not,' the Doctor muttered under his breath, his smile faltering for a second. Then it was back and he was off again. 'So you must be the one in charge around here. Excellent! Excellent. And that would be Captain...?' The Doctor left the question hanging.

'Bartholomew,' the Captain replied gruffly, sizing the Doctor up now as if he were an eager young cabin boy. 'And yes, the Venture is my ship, but you're mistaken about one thing; I'm not in charge.'

'That would be me,' the other man said archly, staring intently at the three stowaways. His expression softened when it fell upon Amy.

'And you would be?' the Doctor asked.

'Proudfoot. Sir Solomon Proudfoot,' the man announced in a upper class English accent. He looked every part the Victorian explorer.

'Proudfoot by name and' – the Doctor glanced at the man's highly polished shoes – 'Proudfoot by nature. And a bow tie!' the Time Lord announced eyeing the explorer's choice of neckwear.

He turned to companions. 'I told you bow ties were cool.'

'Yeah, right,' Amy said. 'They're right up there with Stetsons and fezzes.'

The Doctor met the gentleman's scrutinizing gaze once more.

'So what are you doing out here in the middle of the' – the Doctor leaned forward, so that he might get a better look at the maps spread out on the table top – 'Gulf of Mexico?'

'The Gulf of Mexico?' Rory gasped. 'You're

rather a long way from home, aren't you?'

'I might ask you the same thing, Doctor,' Captain Bartholomew retorted, cutting Rory dead with a sharp look.

'Yes, you well might, but I asked first,' the Doctor said with a grin.

'We are undertaking an expedition of the utmost importance,' Sir Solomon said. 'A vital mission into untamed lands.'

'Would you mind telling me what the time is?' the Doctor suddenly asked, rocking back on his heels.

'Why,' Proudfoot said, taking a fob watch on a chain from a pocket in his waistcoat – something in the Doctor's tone compelling him to obey without him even realising it – 'it's about half past eight.'

'Sorry, could you be more specific?' the Doctor said, checking the watch strapped to his own wrist now.

The gentleman checked his timepiece again. 'Eight twenty-seven a.m.'

'Even more specific than that?'

'More specific than eight twenty-seven?'

'I mean, what year is it?'

'What year?' Captain Bartholomew echoed in disbelief. 'Why it's the Year of Our Lord Eighteen Hundred and Eighty-One, of course. Where have you been that you don't know what year it is?'

'Oh, places you wouldn't believe!' the Doctor said.

'Er, I hope you don't mind me asking,' Amy piped up, 'but aren't you just the teensiest bit curious as to what we're doing on-board your ship?'

'She's got a point, you know.' the Doctor said, smiling broadly at the captain and the expedition leader.

Sir Solomon Proudfoot opened his mouth, as if about to answer, a mystified expression on his face. But before he could do so, a shuddering clang rocked the ship. The tramp steamer had collided with something. Something big.

Amy was immediately reminded of the collision that had occurred within the Vortex, and that had resulted in the TARDIS being forced to crash-land on-board the tramp steamer in the first place.

Everyone instinctively grabbed hold of something so that they weren't thrown across the cabin by the collision. The captain and Sir Solomon hung onto the chart table, as did the Doctor. Amy seized the ship's wheel. The bosun clung onto a length of iron pipework, his muscles tensing.

Rory failed to grab hold of anything and grunted as he fell against a pressure gauge. He doubled up on the floor, his face contorted by pain.

'What was that?' Amy demanded.

'Come on!' the Doctor declared, springing into action and throwing himself at the door. 'Let's go see!'

Before the burly bosun could stop him, he was through. The Nigerian hesitated for a moment, throwing a desperate glance towards his captain, and then set off after the Doctor, gun in hand.

'You too!' Amy snapped, grabbing Rory by the hand. Dragging him after her she set off after the Doctor and the burly Mr Hayes.

The Doctor was already halfway across the deck. He was heading for the port bow. A cluster of crewmen were already there, peering over the rusting gunwales of the ship at the seething sea below.

Amy and Rory joined the Doctor and the sailors as a blunt-headed monster erupted from the churning waters. It was all fangs and fury, and ready to consume them all.

CHAPTER FIVE
THAR SHE BLOWS!

The time travellers and the sailors threw themselves backwards as the huge jaws snapped shut, catching nothing but empty air.

Amidst the spray Amy glimpsed a huge dark shape. For a moment it seemed to blot out the sun. And then the thing was falling again, hitting the sea with a huge splash that threw another crashing wave across the deck of the tramp steamer.

As the sailors backed away from the edge of the ship, the Doctor – his hair and clothes soaked through by the sudden tsunami – leapt to his feet and was at the gunwale again in seconds. Leaning out over the side of the ship it looked like he might actually dive into the ocean after the monster.

Unable to conquer her own curiosity, Amy joined him. Her husband was there at her side a moment later although he was noticeably less enthusiastic.

'What was that?' Amy asked, scouring the churning waters on the port side of the ship. 'Was that what we hit?'

'I can't be certain,' the Doctor said, 'but I think –'

Before he could finish whatever it was he was going to say, the Doctor suddenly climbed onto the gunwale. Supporting himself with a hand around one of the steel cables that connected to the mast he pointed at the sea with a furious stabbing finger. 'Thar she blows!'

Amy and Rory looked. Fifty metres out from the boat a dark silhouette moved beneath the waters with all the menace of a circling shark. Only it wasn't a shark, Amy was certain of that.

'What is it?' Rory demanded, his voice wavering. 'I mean it has to be – what? – at least thirty metres long!'

'I know,' said the Doctor, his voice almost a whisper, 'fantastic, isn't it?'

With a sudden flick of its tail, the submerged creature turned sharply and began to swim back towards the Venture, great paddle-like flippers pulling it through the water. As it came closer, the bright morning sunlight penetrating the water revealed a hide dappled blue and grey. A ridged spine ran the length of its back and its head alone had to be the size of one of the Venture's lifeboats. It was a truly awesome sight. And it was heading right for the ship.

'You beauty!' the Doctor gasped, in delight.

'So what is it, Doctor?' Amy asked again. 'I mean, apart from some kind of terrible sea monster?'

'It's an adult Liopleurodon,' the Doctor said, grinning like a schoolboy.

'A Lio-what?' Amy said. She was unable to take her eyes off the leviathan slicing through the sea towards them.

'It's a dinosaur, isn't it?' Rory butted in. 'What

you're trying to say is that there's a dinosaur about to attack the ship. Isn't that right, Doctor?'

The Doctor shot the young man a delighted smile. 'Fabulous, isn't it?'

Rory looked at the Doctor, his mouth open in amazement which was slowly turning into a smile all of his own.

'Course it is!' The Doctor turned back to his observation of the approaching sea monster. 'Liopleurodon Saevus, a prehistoric predator that called the warm shallow seas of the Mesozoic era home,' he went on. 'The middle Jurassic to be precise.'

'But I thought this was supposed to be 1881,' Rory pointed out.

'That was what the Captain said,' Amy agreed.

'Then what's a dinosaur doing in the Caribbean in 1881?'

'Looks like the crawl to me,' the Time Lord said, a twinkle in his eye.

'What?'

'Sorry, couldn't resist,' the Doctor replied. 'And

besides, it's the Gulf of Mexico, not the Caribbean; you're a couple of hundred miles out.'

Rory scowled. 'Well, I suppose if you're going to dress like a geography teacher…'

'I bet the creature's being here has got something to do with the time fracture the TARDIS detected when we landed,' the Doctor went on, ignoring Rory's last comment.

'Time fracture?' Amy said. 'Like the crack in my bedroom wall?'

'Yes, but no. Not that time fracture. Not a crack in the skin of the universe.'

Amy's anxious expression softened in relief.

'So what's causing this one?' Rory asked.

'Again with the good questions. You don't miss a trick, do you, Rory? But it's actually 'these' if we're being precise. There's more than one.'

'It's coming round again!' the bosun's booming voice came from behind them.

'Ready weapons, take aim and prepare to fire on my mark!' he commanded the crew. The sailors were even now rallying at the bow, taking up whatever weapons they had to hand.

'What?' the Doctor exclaimed, spinning round. His feet teetered on the edge of the ship. 'No! No guns!' he commanded, waving the approaching crewmen away. 'I will not allow it! You will not harm this beautiful creature.'

From his position on the deck, Mr Hayes looked from the sea monster to the Doctor and back again. His features were set hard and he was still tracking the Liopleurodon's approach with the pistol in his hand.

'It won't attack you if you don't attack it first,' the Doctor told the wavering crewmen.

'But it's attacked us once already!'

Captain Bartholomew's voice rang out across the deck, over the crash of the waves and the twang of the wind in the ship's cables. Such was the power of the Captain's words, and the respect he commanded from his crew, that many of those present turned their eyes from the leviathan to face him.

'You don't know that!' the Doctor insisted.

'How can you say that?' Sir Solomon Proudfoot demanded, standing at the Captain's side on the deck outside the cabin.

'The collision could have been an accident,' the Doctor said. 'Pure chance.'

'Or it could have been protecting its territory,' Rory suggested.

'Look, Rory, you're not helping,' the Doctor hissed.

'Well accident or no, we're in its territory,' Captain Bartholomew stated darkly, 'and now it's angry.'

All eyes turned back to the sleek shadow sliding through the water with all the speed of a motorboat. There could be no doubt now as to its intention now.

The monster was on a collision course with the ship.

CHAPTER SIX
LEVIATHAN

'**H**old fire!' the Doctor commanded.

The sailors craned their heads to see more clearly as the monster's blunt snout came within reach of the ship once more.

The sound of several weapons been primed echoed across the deck. Mr Hayes' weapon was amongst them. 'I said hold your fire!' the Doctor roared.

An uneasy stillness descended over the deck of the rocking ship. The only sounds Amy could hear were the splash of the waves against the hull and the deep, throbbing rumble coming from the ship's engine room somewhere below deck.

The Doctor remained frozen, balanced on the gunwale of the ship, as the ancient leviathan drew alongside the Venture.

But rather than attack, this time the beast dived and slid under the hull of the ship. It left all those watching from on deck in no doubt as to just how vast it was and the potential power locked within its monstrous form.

The Doctor, Amy and Rory – along with the explorer Proudfoot, Captain Bartholomew and all his crew – watched as the beast passed beneath the tramp steamer. The expressions on some of the sailors' faces suggested that they were half expecting the monster to surface whilst under the boat.

Amy's mind filled with doubts. Perhaps the creature was indeed planning on tipping them all into the sea. If they ended up in the water it would be able to finish them off with ease.

'We're going to need a bigger boat,' Rory breathed.

An appalling grating sound shuddered through

the ship. There was a sharp intake of breath from all those on deck as the liopleurodon's ridged back scraped the barnacles from the ship's keel.

A moment later the monster appeared on the other side of the steamer. The crew hurried across the deck after it, keen not to lose sight of the beast, preferring to know exactly where it was at all times.

The Doctor let out a sigh of relief.

'You were right,' Amy said. She watched as the monster zigzagged through the water, all muscle and menace.

'Yes, that was lucky, wasn't it?' the Doctor said, sounding almost as surprised as his companion.

'Right, we haven't got a moment to lose.' He jumped down from his perch on the gunwale and was suddenly racing back towards the bridge.

'We need to get away from this spot as quickly as we can, while we still can, before that beauty changes its mind!' he called to Captain Bartholomew.

'Since when did the captain of the Venture start taking orders from stowaways?' the captain growled.

'You said it yourself. We're in what the Liopleurodon considers to be its territory. Think of that last swim past as a shot across the bows. It's giving you the chance to turn round and get out of here, and if I were you I'd make the most of the opportunity and skedaddle. Ooh, skedaddle. That's a word I haven't used in a long time. Skedaddle!'

'Doctor?' Amy said through gritted teeth.

'Oh yes, sorry. Where was I? Oh, that's right. Captain Bartholomew, I believe you were about to give the order?'

'Back to your stations!' the Captain shouted. The crew scattered at his command.

'Now, I want you to follow the bearing I'm going to give you,' the Doctor had to shout to be heard over the hubbub of activity that had suddenly broken out on deck. As he ran, he pulled the crushed raffle ticket from his pocket.

'And what bearing would that be, Doctor?' the Captain demanded.

'Again with the orders,' Amy muttered, watching Captain Bartholomew anxiously.

The Time Lord consulted the scrap of paper in his hand, turned it the right way up and checked it again. Whipping out a silver and bronze pen-like device he depressed a switch on its side. The end of the device sprang open like some rare metallic flower and it began to emit a high-pitched buzzing whine.

'Well, to put it simply,' he said, turning and pointing back beyond the dipping prow of the ship, 'that way.'

Amy and Rory followed the Doctor's finger and saw, on the distant horizon, a dark green line of vegetation. It was land; it had to be.

'Well that's handy, isn't it?' Captain Bartholomew replied, his voice low and menacing. 'Because that's the way we're already headed.'

The liopleurodon was almost out of sight now as it continued to course backwards and forwards through the sea like a cross between a giant crocodile and the Loch Ness Monster.

'And, just out of interest, what do you expect to find when you get to wherever it is you're going?'

the Doctor asked, whilst avoiding the captain's stony gaze.

An eerie silence descended over the Venture at that one innocent remark.

Amy turned. A lone figure was emerging from the throng of crewmen milling about the deck, the sailors moving out of his way as he passed by.

He looked old. His arms were thin, his legs spindly and his skin was the colour of old leather. His clothes were little better than rags. He looked like a scarecrow. His face was lined with wrinkles while on top of his head he was wearing a scuffed and scratched pith helmet. An untidy handlebar moustache, the colour of sun-bleached seashells, bristled from his top lip.

'Nice hat!' the Doctor remarked.

The strange old man peered at the Doctor and his companions from beneath beetling brows.

'We're headed into the unknown,' he said. There was a strange, sing-song quality to his voice. Amy wondered if he was suffering from sunstroke.

'The unknown, that's the ticket!' the Doctor

exclaimed, clapping his hands together and spinning on his heel. 'How exciting!'

'We're searching for the fountain,' the old man continued.

'What fountain?' Amy asked, moving herself closer to the Doctor.

'What fountain?' the old man chuckled. 'What fountain? Why, the fountain, of course. The fountain of legend. Ponce de León's prize.'

'Poncey who?' Rory butted in.

The old man suddenly turned on the young man, a manic gleam in his beady black eyes.

'The Fountain of Youth!'

CHAPTER SEVEN
ISHMAEL

The Doctor looked the old man up and down, clearly intrigued and enchanted by this raggedy individual.

'The Fountain of Youth, eh?' he said, the sparkle in his own ancient eyes mirroring the glint of mania in this strange character's spritely gaze. 'And who might you be?'

'Ishmael Cain, sah!' the old man saluted, pulling himself up to his full height of five-foot-nothing. Amy put a hand to her mouth to stop herself from giggling. He looked far too stringy and bony to have ever been a soldier.

'Very good,' the Doctor said.

'I already know who you are, sah!'

'You do?' There was a note of surprise in his voice.

'Oh yes, sah! You're the Doctor!'

'That's right. I think I said as much when we first arrived.' The Doctor eyed the circle of sailors slowly closing around them.

'But that's just it, isn't it Doctor?' the mad old man went on. 'Where did you and the good lady and gentleman arrive from?'

At this Amy and Rory shared wary glances with each other. She had thought it strange that no one on-board the Victorian tramp steamer had asked where they had come from before.

'You sail your blue ship on stranger tides than these, setting your course by other stars than those we know,' the old man said, waving his hands wildly at the cloudless blue sky above.

'Is that so?' the Doctor replied, captivated by the crazed pith helmet-wearing prophet now. 'And how would you know that?'

Ishmael Cain stepped forward and leaned in

close to the Doctor. In what was little more than a husky whisper he said, 'Same way I know what's really going on around here,' and tapped his nose with a finger.

'And what is going on around here?' the Doctor muttered in return.

'They came out of the storm,' Ishmael whispered, conspiratorially, 'on wings of fi–'

'Ishmael!' the Captain's strident tones carried across the deck. 'Leave our guests in peace.'

Shooting the bristle-bearded Bartholomew an anxious look, the old man retreated back into the throng of sailors without saying another word.

Turning, Amy caught sight of the cruel expression on the Captain's face.

'And the rest of you, back to work. We have our heading.'

Amy found herself unable to take her eyes off the strange, sun-crazed old man. He looked like he could have stepped out of the pages of Treasure Island or Robinson Crusoe. If it wasn't for the fact that he was on-board the tramp steamer she might have taken him for a castaway.

'I was just thinking the same thing,' the Doctor said, suddenly there at her shoulder.

'What?' she asked.

'Where they picked that one up from, of course,' he replied, peering from below his floppy fringe at the retreating Ishmael.

'Oh, is that right?' Amy countered.

'That, and what must have happened for him to end up like that.'

CHAPTER EIGHT

WELCOME TO FLORIDA

Its boiler fire well stoked and its engine chugging away furiously, the Venture ploughed a furrow through the rolling waves. Leaving the massive Mesozoic marine predator patrolling the warm waters of the Gulf of Mexico, the ship headed east. An ever-expanding line of trees was now clearly visible on the horizon.

As the sun reached its highest point in the heavens at noon, the tramp steamer made it to the shallower waters off the coast. Once there, Captain Bartholomew at last gave the order for the crew to weigh anchor.

The Doctor was leaning out over the prow of

the ship, arms outstretched looking like he was he was about to take a dive into the crystal clear waters below. 'Ladies and gentlemen!' he announced with great gusto. 'Welcome to Florida!'

'Florida?' Amy and Rory gasped.

'Where did you think we were going?' The mop-haired man turned, presenting them with a broad grin. 'Where else would you find the fabled Fountain of Youth?'

'Yeah, I've been meaning to ask you about that,' Rory piped up. It had been all hands on deck since the Captain had said the three stowaways could stay. After some debate with his employer Sir Solomon Proudfoot, he had declared that they would have to work their passage. There had hardly been time to catch breath, never mind to waste it in idle chit-chat. 'I mean what's the deal there? I've heard of it, of course, along with Blackbeard –'

'Did I ever tell you that I met him once?' the Doctor interrupted.

'Who? Blackbeard?'

'Well, one version of him.'

'You're name-dropping again, Doctor,' Amy said, scolding him with a smile.

'Anyway, back to the Fountain of Youth,' Rory said pointedly. 'It really does exist then, does it?'

'Does it?' the Doctor said, his smile broadening.

'Come on, Doctor. A simple 'yes' or 'no' would do.'

'We'll just have to wait and see for ourselves, won't we?'

'You really think it could be out there, Doctor?' Amy asked.

'Why not? All legends have some basis in fact. I'll bet you didn't used to believe in vampires, or homo reptilia, or the power of dreams, or shape-changers,' he said, looking from one to the other with a twinkle in his eye, 'but you do now, don't you?'

'Yes, of course,' Rory said. 'After what we've seen how could we not?'

'Then the Fountain of Youth could well exist too. At least, there could be something lurking at the heart of the Everglades doing a very good impression of a Fountain of Youth.'

'And Proudfoot thinks he's going to find it here?' Amy said.

'Well, why not? I mean reports go back centuries about a magical spring that restores the youth of anyone who drinks of its waters. Herodotus wrote about it, and it appears in the stories of Prester John. According to one legend, the Spanish explorer Juan Ponce de León was searching for it when he travelled to Florida in the sixteenth century – although it wasn't called that then, of course – so why shouldn't it be there?'

'Have you never thought to look for it yourself, Doctor?' Rory asked.

'Nah,' the Doctor replied, running a hand through his tousled mop of dark hair. 'I mean when you've lived for centuries already and have the ability to regenerate every cell in your body –'

'The ultimate face-lift,' Amy said with a smile.

'– then a mythical fountain that restores your youth doesn't seem like such a novelty.'

'I went to Florida once, when I was six. My parents took me to Disneyworld,' Rory said.

'Really?' the Doctor said, although it was clear to Amy that he wasn't really listening.

'Yeah. Couldn't get my head round how big the mouse was. Freaked me out.'

'Well I doubt you'll be seeing many mice this time around,' the Doctor said, examining his sonic screwdriver intently.

'How come?'

'The pythons and alligators will have eaten all the mice, I expect.'

'Not to mention any other prehistoric monsters that might just happen to be hanging out in the jungle,' Amy said.

'Not jungle – mangrove swamps,' the Doctor corrected her. 'They really are quite beautiful, you know? Dripping with orchids.'

'Whatever. Anyway, what are the chances it's all going to be just a teensy bit Jurassic Park in there?'

'I preferred The Land that Time Forgot,' Rory threw in.

'What?'

'It's a classic. Stop motion, none of your

soulless CGI. I used to love watching the re-runs on Sunday afternoon telly.'

'Well it's a good thing you've got us to keep you entertained now, isn't it?' Amy laughed, putting her arm through his. 'So what now, Doctor?'

'Now, we go ashore,' Sir Solomon Proudfoot said.

The Doctor and his companions turned. The explorer was advancing across the deck behind them.

'All of us?' Rory asked.

'But of course,' Proudfoot said, making his way over to the side of the steamer. Some of the crew were already lowering a lifeboat into the water. The explorer pointed at the crates and canvas bags that had been loaded into it. 'Who's going to carry all this otherwise?'

Amy caught the gleam in his eye as one corner of his mouth curled upwards.

She skipped over to the edge of the ship, dragging Rory with her, eager to be one of the first to disembark.

'Hang on,' she said, stopping abruptly. She looked down at herself.

She was wearing a vintage bomber jacket, denim shorts and her sleeveless tan top. Glancing up again she met Sir Solomon's gaze as well as that of her husband.

'I'm not really dressed for jungle trekking, am I?'

'None of us are,' the Doctor said, squeezing past all of them.

'But do you think I could just pop back to the TARDIS and change?'

'We'll miss the boat if we have to wait for you to choose a new outfit,' Rory threw in.

The Doctor snorted with laughter.

Amy scowled at them both.

'He's right you know.' Amy's scowl deepened. 'What?' the Doctor protested. 'I was only making an observation. Don't have a go at me – I'm not your husband,' before adding under his breath, 'thank goodness.'

'What did you say?' Amy snapped.

'My, is that the time?' the Doctor announced,

suddenly peering at the watch strapped to his wrist with unusual interest. 'Come on, we sail with the tide! And you know what they say about time and the tide.'

'They wait for no man?' Amy offered.

'That's right, and they're not going to wait for you either, Pond, so get in that boat.'

CHAPTER NINE
READY WHEN YOU ARE

Practically everyone on-board The Venture, other than Captain Bartholomew and a few Chinese ratings, piled into three of the steamship's lifeboats that had already been winched down into the water.

Sir Solomon Proudfoot boarded the first boat, along with various members of the crew. The men had to squeeze themselves in between the wooden crates and all manner of camping equipment. It looked like the explorer had packed anything and everything he might need for the expedition ahead.

Amy, Rory and the Doctor boarded the second boat under the watchful eye of Mr Hayes. It was clear from the bosun's grim expression that he wasn't ready to trust these strange stowaways just yet.

Proudfoot's boat was already negotiating the low reefs and shoals that lay between The Venture and the shore. As Mr Hayes was readying their craft for the off they were joined by Ishmael Cain. He was clutching a mop – one normally used for swabbing the decks – as if it was a rifle and he had his pith helmet pushed down hard on his head.

Squeezing himself into the boat beside the Doctor he called out, 'Ready when you are, Mr Hayes!'

With the sailors pulling hard on the oars, the second lifeboat set off for the shore.

Having also successfully navigated the low rocks of the reef, they followed the first boat up the coast to the point where a wide river estuary joined the sea. From there they headed upstream, into the steamy clutches of the mangrove swamps.

As the trees closed over their heads, they entered the eerie green gloom of the Everglades. Strange chittering and hooting cries echoed between the knotted roots and branches, whilst loud bird calls rang from the forest canopy.

Amy shuffled closer to her husband, taking his arm in hers again. She scanned the densely-packed trees on either side of the river. She thought the sailors looked just as anxious as she was feeling. The Doctor, on the other hand, appeared to be entirely unperturbed. He had one eye on his sonic screwdriver which he was pointing towards the prow of their boat.

'Do you know something?' Ishmael suddenly whispered. His knuckles whitened as he tightened his grip on the imaginary rifle he was holding.

'And what's that?' Amy asked, happy to have something else to distract her for a moment.

Her nose wrinkled. The old man smelt of salt and stale sweat.

'Do you know what the old mapmakers used to write on their maps of this region, on their charts of the Florida peninsula?'

'No, what?'

Ishmael glanced left and right, as if worried that something beyond the boat, lurking in the green gloom, might overhear him, before finally fixing Amy and Rory with a piercing stare.

'Here be dragons!'

CHAPTER TEN
UPSTREAM

Amy and Rory spent the last leg of the journey upriver in silence. They continued to scan the forest beyond the banks of the river, half expecting a dragon – or something very much like one – to burst from the jungle roaring, ready to devour them all. The Doctor, meanwhile, sat happily chatting with the deranged Ishmael, occasionally checking their course using his sonic screwdriver.

The further they travelled upstream the closer the river's banks came, until they were passing through a winding gorge of water-cut limestone draped with vines. The river itself was becoming faster-flowing and there were more and more rocks visible just beneath the surface. The croaking cries of birds ringing through the trees were drowned by the roar of white water as the three lifeboats drew nearer to the boulder-strewn rapids.

The churning cascades created a natural barrier that prevented the expedition from travelling any further by boat. Sir Solomon Proudfoot ordered that they put into the shore and secure the boats before unloading them, ready to continue on foot. Whatever it was that was inside the wooden crates was carefully transferred into backpacks. These were then hoisted onto the backs of the sailors and one was even given to Rory. When it was Amy's and the Doctor's turn to get loaded up, there weren't any backpacks left.

Once all was ready, the party continued on its winding way, ever deeper into the primeval landscape. Sir Solomon led the way, machete in hand, hacking a path through the undergrowth. He was joined by two other crewmen who also set about attacking the forest with powerful swipes of their heavy knives.

Fat insects laboured through the humid air. The cloying atmosphere was thick with the peaty smells of rotting vegetable matter and damp earth.

Already soaked in sweat, Amy had taken off her jacket and tied it around her waist. Rory had done the same with his winter vest, securing it to the belt on his trousers. Sweat dripped from the faces of the men hacking a path through the forest. Proudfoot was forced to stop regularly in order to wipe the perspiration from his eyes so that he could see where he was going.

Nobody spoke; the heat sapped their energy. It was hard enough simply to keep walking in the prickly heat. They certainly didn't have enough strength left for idle talk.

Only the Doctor seemed unaffected by the heat, although even he had slung his jacket over one shoulder and rolled up his shirt sleeves.

Sir Solomon had rolled up his sleeves too and Amy couldn't help but notice the strange copper-coloured bracelet he wore on his left wrist. She wondered if it was a relic he had picked up during a previous adventure.

It felt to Amy like they had been walking for hours when the smothering undergrowth parted at last and they found themselves walking across a valley basin. The natural bowl it formed in the landscape was a lush pasture. Thick fern fronds rose to knee height between well-spaced spindly palms.

'Look,' the Doctor said. He was gazing around the humid forest with child-like wonder. 'Epiphytes.'

'Bless you,' Amy said automatically.

The Time Lord scowled and pointed. A mass of fern-like leaves and brilliant red and purple flowers were growing from cracks in the bark of a cypress tree. 'No, I mean look at those bromeliads.'

'And again. You've really got it bad, haven't you, Doctor?'

'What is it,' chuckled Rory, 'hay fever?'

'We're getting closer,' Ishmael muttered. His voice was little more than a harsh whisper that only the Doctor and his companions could hear.

'Closer to the fountain?' Rory whispered back.

'He's right, you know,' the Doctor said, checking the readings on his sonic screwdriver again.

'How do you know?' Rory asked Ishmael.

'I can feel it,' Ishmael replied in answer to Rory's question. 'In here,' he added, tapping his head with a wizened, claw-like finger.

'What was that?' Amy hissed.

Everyone froze.

'Can you feel that too, or is it just me?'

She could feel the ground shuddering beneath her feet.

'No, Pond, it's not just you,' the Doctor said, shooting wary glances in all directions around the vast clearing.

'There!' someone suddenly shouted from the head of the line. 'Up ahead!'

Ishmael made a noise at the back of his throat like a wet leopard growl.

'Something's coming,' he said.

CHAPTER ELEVEN
OCCUPATIONAL HAZARD

It was as if the jungle had come to life, the trees and bushes in front of them shaking violently.

With a wet splintering sound, a pair of saplings came crashing down and the first of the animals burst from the forest.

Crashing through the undergrowth towards them was a beast the size of a tank and with the armour to match. Its mottled green and brown hide was rough and knobbly. But it was the array of plates lined up along its back and heavily-spiked tail that made it instantly recognisable.

Amy remained exactly where she was as the creature charged towards them. The huge animal opened its beaked mouth and gave a sonorous hooting bellow. Proudfoot's party had already broken up as the men attempted to scramble out of its way.

'I know that one,' she gasped, frozen to the spot in shock. 'That's a stegosaurus!'

'So it is,' said the Doctor staring at the heavily-built beast thundering towards them. 'And so's that one, and that one, and that one...'

More of the dinosaurs were emerging from the tree line after the bull stegosaur that was leading the charge. And they kept on coming.

'It's a whole herd!' Rory exclaimed.

Panicking sailors sprinted past them, back the way they had come across the clearing.

'Yes, it would rather appear that way,' the Doctor said, 'and they're coming this way. So, if I were you, I'd start running. Come on, Doctor's orders!'

'What is it with you and running?' Amy muttered, nonetheless doing as the Doctor told her.

'Occupational hazard,' he said, beginning to

pick up the pace.

'I've been wondering, Doctor,' Rory gasped as they ran, 'have you ever thought about running the London Marathon?'

'Oh no,' the Doctor called back, sonic in one hand, his jacket in the other. 'Imagine it. Running for three or four hours? In one go? I'd get bored far too quickly.'

'Stop talking, boys, and run!' Amy shouted. She glanced back over her shoulder. 'They're getting closer!'

'These boots really weren't made for running,' she added to herself. 'I dressed for the Renaissance, not for running through the jungle being chased by dinosaurs!'

'That tree!' the Doctor said, pointing to the low-hanging branches of another cypress. 'Get climbing!'

Amy and Rory didn't need to be told twice. Amy reached the tree first. The rest of the expedition continued back down the track they had cut through the forest, heading for what little cover the undergrowth there might provide.

Grabbing a branch, Amy pulled herself up. Desperation lent her the strength she needed. Kicking at the trunk to help get a purchase, she made it to the relative safety of the higher branches. From her perch she lent down to help her husband, the Doctor forming a stirrup with his hands for Rory to step into.

With the two of them no longer in danger of being trampled by the charging stegosaurs, Amy and Rory both stretched a hand down to help the Doctor.

'Here, take this,' the Time Lord said, tossing Amy his precious sonic screwdriver so that he might get a better grip on the tree himself.

Amy snatched it from the air as it tumbled end over end towards her. As she did, she caught sight of the charging dinosaurs again.

'Doctor, hurry!' she screamed as he tried to climb up after them. The stegosaurs were bearing down on him like a fleet of bulldozers.

He was a tangle of gangly limbs. He reached

for Rory's outstretched hand only to lose his grip on the mossy branch he was already clinging onto.

As the bellowing bull at the head of the herd thundered past beneath them its heaving flanks scraped against the tree. The cypress shook so hard Amy feared the dinosaur might bring it crashing down altogether.

With a startled cry the Doctor fell.

His cry of surprise was cut off abruptly as he landed on top of the beast, caught between the triangular fin-like plates on its back. He gave a breathless, 'Oomph!'

Straddling the animal's neck, there was nothing he could do as it thundered on through the forest. The rest of the herd following the bull, the ground trembled at their passing as if in the grip of an earthquake.

As Amy and Rory watched, helpless on their perch among the crooked branches, the stegosaurs ploughed back into the dense undergrowth on the other side of the clearing.

The last they heard of the Doctor, was a

delighted cry of 'Geronimo!' as the stegosaur carried him away into the cloying green gloom of the forest.

CHAPTER TWELVE
TERRIBLE LIZARD

'**D**octor!' Amy screamed after the departing dinosaurs, but it was no good – he was already gone. Unable to stop herself she began to cry.

Rory caught her up in his arms, holding her close, the two of them still lodged in the crook of the tree. 'Don't worry,' he said, 'we'll find him. But first we're going to need to get out of this tree.'

Amy wiped her eyes clear of tears and then the two of them clambered down from the tree. Sir Solomon Proudfoot's party was already reassembling in the middle of the clearing.

The explorer was walking across the glade towards them through the swishing ferns. 'Are you alright?' he asked Amy. She couldn't help but notice that he was checking the load of his unholstered pistol as he did so.

'We have to go after those things,' she stated.

'We're fine, thank you,' Rory said.

'Yes, we're fine, but the Doctor won't be if we don't go after those dinos now!'

'We're not going anywhere,' the explorer said, giving her a flint-hard stare. 'Not until we've got everyone back together.'

'And then we go after the Doctor,' Amy persisted.

'No. Then we resume our mission and head for our original objective,' Proudfoot said coldly. 'We'll just have to do our best without him.'

Amy stared at him aghast. 'And what's that supposed to mean? You'd rather head off on some wild goose chase than help another' – she hesitated, before saying – 'human being?'

'It is not some wild goose chase,' Proudfoot snarled.

'But the Doctor is in danger. We have to

help him!'

The explorer's dead-eyed stare continued to bore into her like a laser. 'The Doctor could be useful to us, I'll grant you that, but his well-being is not my concern.'

'I don't believe I'm hearing this!' Amy said.

'We stay together and we stay on course for our original objective,' Proudfoot said. The rest of the Venture's crew had seemingly made it back to the glade all in one piece.

Rory looked from his wife to the explorer and back again. 'Am I the only one wondering why there are even dinosaurs here, in this jungle, in the first place?' he asked, the disbelief clear in his face.

'Well the Doctor's fate is our concern,' Amy said, 'so we're going after him.'

She turned and strode off after the stegosaurs, following the trail the gigantic animals had left behind them. A ten-metre wide passage of flattened ferns and cycads, crushed during the stegosaurs' stampede, stretched across the clearing.

'Are we?' Rory asked, shooting anxious glances

at the trees surrounding the valley basin.

'Yes we are!' his wife retorted, turning on her heel and grabbing his hand. She glared at Sir Solomon Proudfoot, her eyes flashing with green fire.

'Yes, of course we are!' Rory echoed.

'I said, everyone stays together.' Proudfoot's voice was quietly sinister.

Slamming his pistol shut he pointed it straight at Amy's face, his finger tightening on the trigger.

Amy swallowed hard as she heard the click of the weapon being primed.

And then suddenly there was Rory, standing between Proudfoot's gun and his wife. He met the explorer's flinty stare with a furious gaze of silent anger all of his own.

Proudfoot stayed exactly where he was. His gun didn't waver.

Rory slowly turned to face his wife. Amy looked back at him, the fury in her own eyes fading to be replaced by a look of joy. 'You know what they saw about discretion being the better part of valour.'

Amy said nothing.

'Well I think now would be the perfect time to put it into practice.'

Amy held her indignant pose a moment longer and then her shoulders sagged. 'All right,' she said, begrudgingly. 'For now,' she added, throwing Proudfoot another venomous glare.

'That's my girl.'

Rory turned back to address the gun-toting explorer. 'We'll go with you,' he said in a quiet voice that had never sounded more threatening, 'for now. But if you ever point your gun at my wife again –'

Rory's pronouncement died in his throat as a blood-curdling, reptilian roar echoed across the glade. A split second later a tremor passed through the ground at their feet.

As one, Proudfoot and the rest of the expedition party turned to face the tree line, sweeping the emerald shadows lurking between the trees with their guns.

'The stegosaurs!' Amy gasped. 'They're

coming back!'

'No, I don't think so,' Rory said keeping his voice low. 'I think it's something else.'

The thick vegetation was forced apart a second time as something much worse than a herd of stegosaurs burst from the forest into the glade. All muscle and teeth and furious carnivorous hunger, the terrible lizard hesitated. Its huge head swung from side to side, nostrils flaring as it sniffed the air.

The monster strode into the glade on two powerful legs. Its armoured hide was mottled orange and brown, banded with tiger-like stripes of near black across its back. It rippled with the movement of great slabs of muscle underneath. A smaller pair of clawed forelimbs flexed in anticipation of the kill it was about to make.

The monster's blunt head was little more than a massive pair of jaws filled with teeth the size of daggers. It continued to sway from side to side as the creature tasted the air. Tiny eyes of yellow hatred struggled to focus on the curious things now fleeing in panic before its advance. The counter-balance of its massive tail slashed at the foliage behind it in irritation.

It might have lost the herd of herbivores that had led it to this place, but here were some other tasty treats that would help keep its hunger at bay until it caught up with the grazers again.

'Well now we know what those stegosaurs were running from,' Rory said, staring in horror at the mighty beast looming over them.

Primeval savagery and knots of corded muscle the size of ship's cables, stalked towards the panicking crew of the Venture as they turned and fled once more. It held its head low, its mouth open, the thick black barb of muscle that was its tongue tasting their fear.

And then it charged.

CHAPTER THIRTEEN
CARNIVORE

The huge creature darted and weaved across the clearing, displaying greater agility than Amy would have believed possible of something so large.

She had faced down Weeping Angels, the Atraxi and even Daleks, but a fully grown extra from the movie set of King Kong? That was a new one on her.

The creature opened its jaws wider still and gave another shrieking cry that echoed across the glade. Amy fancied she could feel its stinking breath – reeking of rotting meat – rippling through her hair.

'A T-Rex,' she said in a breathless whisper.

'Yes, I can see that,' Rory said, adrenalin rushing through his body, 'but if I might make a suggestion, let's – RUN!'

Not once taking his eyes from the mass of muscle and primeval savagery, Sir Solomon Proudfoot slowly turned his gun away from Rory and Amy, training it instead on the approaching tyrannosaur.

'You can't be serious!' Rory gasped in utter disbelief. 'That thing must have a hide as thick as a rhinoceros. You think a few feeble bullets are going to stop it?'

But Proudfoot kept the gun trained on the beast, as if sizing up his target. The dinosaur took another lumbering step closer, sending more of the Venture's crew scattering before it.

The T-Rex suddenly lunged, head low, and caught one of the desperate men in its cutlass teeth. It was Mr Hayes the bosun.

Throwing back its head, the gigantic predator tossed the yelling sailor into the air before catching him again in its gaping jaws.

Amy turned away before she saw anymore but she still heard the wet crunch of bone as the bosun's screams suddenly ceased.

'Don't be a fool!' Rory said, tugging at the explorer's arm and spoiling his aim. 'You wouldn't have a hope. Save yourself, while you still can!'

'Behold now Behemoth!' Ishmael shouted as he turned and ran.

For a moment it looked like Proudfoot might try to stare down the dinosaur. Then he clearly thought better of it. Deftly holstering his pistol, he turned and joined the others in fleeing for their lives.

Amy's lungs burned with every gasping breath she took. Her heart was pounding so hard she felt as though it might punch through her ribs at any second. She could feel the ground shuddering with every crashing step the dinosaur took. The ferocious carnivore was probably closing on them with every powerful stride.

She could hear the desperate cries and panicked screams of those sailors who were not quick enough to escape. The terrible lizard picked them off, one after another, and Amy heard every chomp as limbs were bitten through.

For around two million years, Tyrannosaurus Rex had been the top predator of the Cretaceous period. A few terrified human beings certainly weren't going to cause this particular specimen any trouble.

Amy wished she could block her ears to save her from the horrible sounds. However, they did encourage her to re-double her efforts as she sprinted across the glade and into the smothering undergrowth beyond the tree- line. Ferns whipped wetly at her legs as she ran back into the jade twilight of the forest.

Perhaps there, in the unnatural green dusk, the T-Rex would lose sight of them. She was sure she had read somewhere once that tyrannosaurs – despite being six tonnes of lethally-evolved killing machine – had notoriously poor eyesight.

As Kryptonite was to Superman, so she hoped short-sightedness was to the T-Rex. There certainly wasn't anyone better placed to put the theory to the test right now than her. What did some palaeontologist studying a fossilized skeleton in the Badlands of Arizona know compared to Amy Pond from Leadworth, who was even now running from a real live T-Rex deep in the Florida Everglades?

A part of her felt almost privileged to be in such a position. In fact, she was sure that some twenty-first century dino-boffins would have died to experience first-hand what it was like to be chased by a hungry tyrannosaur. But then they probably would have died too, taking their knowledge of what it was like to be swallowed by a T-Rex to their graves.

She didn't know where she and the others were running to. She only cared that they were running away from the Tyrannosaur, and as far away as possible at that. She didn't dare stop in case she ended up as dinner for the dinosaur.

She could hear Rory panting behind her. Proudfoot and Ishmael sprinted after him, their flight accompanied by the snap of plant stems and thwack of waxy leaves as they ploughed through the vegetation. The explorer's machete was wholly forgotten now.

The trailing twigs of tree branches and knotty stems whipped at her face and hair. She caught her breath as a thorn, as sharp as a velociraptor's claw, caught her across the right cheek.

She automatically put a hand to the spot. Her fingertips came back red with blood.

Putting up her hands to protect her face she kept running, not slowing her pace once.

She had been dimly aware of the fact that the ground had been rising for some time but suddenly she found herself sprinting up a slope. Her leg muscles burned with the effort, as did the breath in her throat. But she couldn't have stopped even if she'd wanted to – which she didn't.

Just as she was wondering whether they had managed to escape the ravenous beast, Amy heard the thud of falling trees and the splintering of sappy stems coming from behind her. Something very big and very powerful was crashing through the trees after them.

The blood-curdling reptilian roar cut through the emerald depths of the forest once more.

The T-Rex was still on their tail. It might be true that the creature had poor eyesight, but Amy had never read anything about how good this particular carnivore's hearing was, or its sense of smell.

Her thighs feeling like they were on fire, Amy pounded up the slope. She was following a naturally worn animal track that climbed higher between the palms and knotty strangler figs. Over the saurian bellow of the beast pursuing them and the pounding of her own blood in her ears, she could hear another rising roar. It was soon louder than the rest put together.

She suddenly broke through the undergrowth to be greeted by a wide expanse of azure sky. She winced as the late afternoon sunlight hit her. She could see nothing but blue skies from one horizon to the other. Then she looked down.

There before her was an abrupt hundred-metre drop off a sheer cliff.

Amy skidded to a halt, her survival instinct kicking in immediately. She put her arms out to either side to stop herself. It was also a warning to those behind her. A shower of small stones and dry earth went skittering over the edge of the cliff and into the raging void beyond.

A moment later she was joined by her husband. A moment after that the explorer and the wild old man burst from the foliage behind them. They too skidded to a halt before they plunged over the edge and into oblivion.

The roar was a thunderous bellow now. To their right, a crashing torrent of white water poured from the forest to plunge over the waterfall and into the deeply shadowed gorge below. Rainbows danced in the sunlight amidst the crashing spray thrown up by the waterfall, only to fall again like heavy rain.

'Great!' Rory gasped. 'Now what?'

The screeching cry of the T-Rex echoed from

the forest behind them. It sounded closer than ever. It could only be a matter of moments before the monster joined them at the cliff's edge.

'Now?' Amy said, grabbing hold of her husband's hand tightly. 'Now we jump!'

CHAPTER FOURTEEN
GERONIMO!

There wasn't time to think. There was only time to act, otherwise they would never do it. Two long strides took them to the edge of the precipice and then they were treading thin air.

'Geronimo!' Amy shouted as they cleared the cliff.

They dropped like stones, hand in hand, their other hands flapping uselessly at the air, as if that might actually somehow slow their fall. They kept their bodies straight and their feet pointed towards the churning waters of the plunge pool that lay at the bottom of the fern-clad gully.

They hit the water mere seconds later. They

disappeared beneath the surface as a billion silver bubbles broke for the surface around them. And then, with strong kicks, they returned to the surface. Their heads breaking the water, they gasped for breath between spluttering bursts of grateful laughter as Proudfoot and a wailing Ishmael Cain joined them in the river.

Amy's cut stung, but otherwise she was unhurt, despite their dramatic plunge from the top of the waterfall.

A shower of earth and stones splashed into the water around them.

Treading water, Amy pushed her wet hair out of her eyes. Craning her head, she sought the top of the cliff, her eyes fixing on the place they had jumped from only moments before. And there, its massive claws crushing the rock at the edge of the precipice, was their pursuer.

The tyrannosaur was sweeping its head from side to side, snorting loudly as it sniffed the air, searching for their scent.

It was a truly awesome and yet terrifying beast,

Amy thought as she let the current carry her away downstream.

The T-Rex stopped and put its head on one side. Amy was sure that its beady reptilian eye caught sight of the four of them. The super-predator opened its terrible, blood-soaked jaws and bellowed its primeval fury to the skies. But its own primitive instinct for survival prevented it from following them over the edge.

'That was just a little too close for comfort,' Rory said, as he wiped a hand over his face.

'I know what you mean,' Amy agreed, smiling with relief.

'What happened to your cheek?' Rory asked.

'Oh, it's nothing,' Amy said, gently probing the cut again with her fingertips. 'I'll be all right.'

The explorer and Ishmael were spluttering and gasping for breath a few metres behind them. Incredibly, the old man was still holding onto his mop, as if for protection. The current was dragging them all towards the middle of the river, where the flow was fastest.

'I just had a thought,' Rory said.

'And what's that?' Amy asked suspiciously.

'If there are stegosaurs and T-Rexes running around the Everglades, I hate to think what might be in here with us!'

CHAPTER FIFTEEN
WHAT HAPPENED TO THE SKY?

Rory and Amy did their best to hang onto each other as they were carried downstream. The river narrowed as it passed from the plunge pool into the gorge beyond, the force of the water moving rapidly faster and faster. If they had been intending to swim to the river bank and climb out, that moment had already passed. They didn't have a hope of making it to the shore now, not against the full force of the river. The best they could do was to try to keep to the middle of the channel, where the river was deepest, and keep an eye out for submerged boulders.

The explorer and the crazed out man, soaked to the skin like Amy and Rory, bobbed along in the current behind them. Unsurprisingly, somewhere along the way Ishmael Cain had become parted from his pith helmet. The roar of the waterfall gradually faded into the distance behind them. But the primordial roars of rage of the T-Rex continued to echo from the grim walls of the gorge a while longer.

The four of them were carried further and further downstream, having no real idea where they were going. Amy wondered whether they were travelling along on a higher stretch of the same river the expedition had followed into the Everglades. If so it would eventually return them to the spot where they had disembarked from the lifeboats to continue their search for the Fountain of Youth on foot. But before that they would have to negotiate the rapids that had prevented the boats from heading further upstream in the first place.

Amy's thoughts were sharply brought back to the here and now as the fast-flowing river carried them around a sharp bend.

The river vanished abruptly over the edge of another waterfall, not ten metres further on. There was nothing they could do now to escape it either.

'Hold on tight,' she told Rory, holding him close.

They both felt the pull of the current suddenly become even stronger. Then they were tipping over the edge, dropping through the crashing torrent, down into another plunge pool, before being swept away again.

Spluttering and gasping for air, Amy and Rory continued to cling onto one another. Proudfoot and Ishmael followed them over the smaller cascade, Ishmael wailing in terror like a banshee.

The river grew wider, the limestone spur it cut through dropping away to both left and right. The dense forest gradually became a thin line in the distance. Soon it was nothing more than a greeny-brown smudge on the horizon as the river became wider still. Eventually it collected in a vast depression in the landscape where it formed a shallow lake.

The power of the current lessened at last, allowing Amy and Rory to swim to the edge. They pulled themselves out onto the swampy foreshore among clumps of bulrushes and water reeds. Proudfoot followed their lead, as did Ishmael, mop still in hand. They joined them as the couple sat themselves down on the trunk of a fallen tree to catch their breath. Rory was doing his best to wring out his socks, while Amy was trying to comb out her long auburn locks using only her fingers.

'Do you think we'll be safe here?' the explorer asked. He had taken out his pistol, apparently to check that it was still working after its dip in the river.

'That all depends on whether you're planning on pointing your gun at anyone else,' Amy retorted.

Proudfoot glared at her but said nothing. He hadn't even had the good grace to apologise to her yet.

'Surely it won't work after being submerged in river water all that time,' Rory pointed out.

'It'll work,' Proudfoot said.

'Why, is it waterproof or something?'

'Believe me,' the explorer said darkly, 'it'll work.'

Having finished inspecting his gun Proudfoot holstered the weapon once more.

'A-ha!' Ishmael suddenly shouted.

'What? What is it?' Amy demanded. The old man was running back out into the shallows of the lake.

'My pith helmet!' he shouted back joyfully.

The beige helmet was drifting through the water towards the shore. Ishmael swept it up out of the shallows and without even bothering to empty it of river water first, plonked it straight back on his head. 'My helmet!'

'Right,' Proudfoot announced, regaining everyone's attention in an instant. He looked from the burning white disc of the sun in the clear blue sky above to the expanse of water and their place within the unspoiled, primeval landscape. Finally his gaze alighted on Ishmael. 'Which way now?'

'We need to be heading that way.' The old man pointed further along the shore of the shallow lake.

'Oh, really?' Amy said.

The explorer glowered at her again.

'Oh yes,' Ishmael Cain said urgently. ''Cos that way lies the source.'

'The source of what?' Rory asked. 'Do you mean the fabled Fountain of Youth?'

'The source of that, sah.'

Ishmael was pointing across the lake. The rest of them turned to see what it was he was pointing at.

Rory's mouth dropped open in shock. 'What happened to the sky?'

Amy opened her mouth to speak but no words came. She didn't know what to say. There was nothing to say.

The sky had broken.

CHAPTER SIXTEEN
HERE BE DRAGONS

Before they had plunged off the top of the waterfall into the river the sky had been the bluest blue Amy had ever seen. Now it was the colour of a ripe bruise.

And then there was the sun. It was a furious red ball, close to the horizon in front of them. But the sun had been behind them only a moment before. Amy turned to check.

Behind her, beyond the higher land above the limestone gorge, she could see the yellow-white disc low in the sky to the west.

She turned back again. And there was the sun, the colour of molten magma, set within a sky the colour of squid ink.

As she stared at it in disbelief the view seemed to flicker and change. The sky went from purple to blue to orange, back to purple, and then almost black.

Amy finally managed to tear her eyes away from the flickering sky and fixed her husband with a bewildered, hazel-green stare. 'The forest!' she said, her eyes focusing on something over his shoulder.

They all looked again, Rory turning round to see for himself what it was his wife had seen.

There on the horizon, beneath the flickering sky, the landscape was changing too. One moment it was the steaming Everglade forest they had just hacked their way through. Then, a moment later, it looked like an altogether different, darker jungle.

Amy slowly became aware of the fact that the hooting cries of birds and chirrup of insects were being swallowed by the echoing roars and bellows of another age entirely. She was listening to sounds that hadn't been heard in that region for millions of years.

She gave a cry of startled surprise. Someone was standing at her shoulder.

It was Ishmael Cain.

'Here be dragons,' he whispered, not once taking his eyes from the warping jungle.

'We're close,' Sir Solomon Proudfoot said, without offering anything else by way of explanation. Shouldering his pack, he set off through the quagmire of the lake shore, heading for the distorting primeval forest that lay under the ever-shifting sky.

'What about your friends?' Amy called after him.

'What about them?' Proudfoot growled, not breaking his stride.

'Aren't you going to wait for them?'

'And why would I want to do that?'

Ishmael remained where he was. He looked from Rory and Amy to the retreating Proudfoot and then back again.

'So what do we do now?' Rory said. It was

suddenly very clear that the only person who even came close to having the means to defend them from whatever the Cretaceous might spring on them next was walking away towards the heart of the temporal disturbance.

There wasn't any sign that any of the other sailors had survived their encounter with the Tyrannosaur. Even if they had escaped its fury, there was no guarantee they were anywhere near the lost lake.

'We follow Dr Livingstone over there,' Amy said in a disgruntled tone, nodding towards the departing Proudfoot.

'Really?' Rory said, secretly relieved. 'I mean good. Good thinking.'

'The Doctor and this guy were both headed in the same direction,' Amy pointed out, 'remember? If the Doctor's managed to get away from those stegosaurs I bet he'll be doing his best to get to the same place.'

'Again, another good point.' Shooting the colour-changing sky to the east another wary look

Rory said, 'Right you are then. Time's a-wasting, so let's get going.'

Amy and Rory set off after the determined Victorian adventurer, with Ishmael trotting after them.

The mud sucked at their feet but it was easier going this way than it was struggling through the stifling depths of the forest.

A dragonfly as big as a parrot hummed past them, dancing over the pools of still water at the lake's edge, its iridescent eyes and stained glass wings glittering like jewels in the inconstant light.

'What did I say?' Ishmael announced triumphantly. 'Here be dragons!'

They followed the lake shore as it curved round past a stand of looming palms. It seemed to Amy as if the sky was changing colour faster than ever. The sometimes-forest sometimes-jungle continued to warp so she couldn't be certain where, or even when, any of them were now.

And then suddenly they all stumbled to a halt, their feet sloshing in the mud of the lake's edge.

'Oh my!' Rory gasped.

'We've found it!' the explorer declared.

'The Fountain of Youth!' Ishmael shouted, taking his pith helmet off and throwing it into the air in delight.

There, half-sunk in the shallows of the lake, was the object of Sir Solomon Proudfoot's quest.

At first glance it looked like some strange and primitive sculpture, left behind by a forgotten civilisation and now smothered with vines. It was shaped like a huge cube of stone, each side roughly four metres in length. Some of the vines had been cleared away and Amy could see that what she had first taken to be time-worn granite actually looked more like some kind of corroded metal.

Sitting on top of the curious artefact, looking right as rain and happy as a sand boy, was a bedraggled geography teacher with a mop of slicked back dark hair.

'Doctor?' said Amy.

'Evening all,' the Doctor replied. 'What kept you?'

CHAPTER SEVENTEEN
MR AND MRS POND

'What kept us?' Amy exclaimed. 'How about six tonnes of T-Rex?'

She was delighted to see the Doctor but at the same time felt furious for all the worry he had put her through.

'But you're all right now, I see,' the Doctor flashed her a cheerful grin. 'Mr Pond,' he added, saluting the sodden Rory.

Apparently unconcerned by what the Doctor was doing, Sir Solomon Proudfoot approached the cube, Ishmael following behind uncertainly.

A burst of raucous laughter suddenly escaped the Doctor's mouth.

'What's so funny?' Amy demanded, flicking a stray strand of wet red hair out of her face.

'It's just that the name Mr and Mrs Pond has never suited you more!'

Rory finished squeezing the water out of the corner of his winter vest and fixed the Doctor with a hard stare.

'Okay. Perhaps that's not as funny as I first thought,' the Time Lord added under his breath. 'Anyway. Pond,' he said, holding out a hand. 'Screwdriver!'

Amy gasped. In all the excitement of their flight from the T-Rex and their dunking in the river, it had slipped her mind that the Doctor had given her the precious device before being carried off on the back of a stegosaur. For a second she felt a knot of cold panic grip her stomach. What had she done with it? And, even if she still had it, had the screwdriver survived their hectic journey over the waterfall and into the river.

'You have still got it, haven't you?'

Had she? Amy desperately tried to recall what

she had done with the thing since snatching it out of the air when the Doctor had thrown it to her.

When she had been in the tree she had put it the sonic in her jacket pocket. But the jacket had ended up tied around her waist. And then she remembered, and her panicked pulse relaxed again.

'Got it right here,' she said with false bravado, reaching into the pocket of her shorts. She took out the bronze and silver pen-like instrument with a flourish. 'Ta da!'

She casually tossed it up to where the Doctor sat, balanced on top of the curious corroded metal cube.

The Doctor deftly snatched it out of the air. The tip of the device sprang open at the flick of a switch, sending a spray of water droplets flying into the Doctor's face, making him blink.

'What have you been doing with it?' he asked, sounding nonplussed. 'Picking locks underwater?'

'Look here, mister,' Amy replied. 'You're lucky you've got it back at all!'

The Doctor settled for a 'Harrumph!' as he

continued to look over his sonic screwdriver, checking it for water damage. He pressed a button and after an uncertain start, a familiar whirring hum rose from the device. 'Hmm… Well it seems okay, I suppose,' the Doctor admitted.

Without saying another word the Time Lord directed the device at the metal cube and the sonic began to hum repeatedly.

Proudfoot was running his hands over its corroded surface whilst examining the obscured markings that covered it. 'It's intact,' he breathed with obvious relief.

With both the explorer and the Doctor deeply absorbed in what they were doing, Rory and Amy were left standing there, effectively twiddling their thumbs. They were soaking wet and fed up. Their clothes refused to dry out in the humid air, and they had nothing better to do than to gaze in wonder and confusion at the flickering sky above and the fluctuating forest beyond.

Amy started, Ishmael Cain suddenly at her side again.

'Behold! He comes with clouds,' the mad old man muttered. On the far horizon vast black storm clouds were massing. As big as Himalayan crags and lit by crackling bursts of distant lightning they made Amy suddenly feel very small.

Thunder rumbled across the broken sky, with the sound of boulders tumbling down a mountain side.

'And I heard a voice from heaven,' Ishmael went on, 'as the voice of many waters, and as the voice of a great thunder.'

'So,' Amy said, moving away from the babbling old man, 'aren't you going to tell us how you got here first – wherever 'here' is. And aren't you going to tell us what you're up to, seeing as you clearly already know what's going on?'

'Oh, yes, okay,' the Doctor blustered. 'Well, where to start?'

'How about at the beginning?' Rory suggested.

'Oh no, that would take far too long,' the Doctor said. 'You do know I'm over nine hundred years old, don't you? I've been doing this' – he waved at the world around him with his sonic screwdriver, as if casually taking in the whole of creation in doing so – 'for centuries!'

'Cut to the chase, Doctor. Obviously he means take it from the point where you rode off into the sunset on the back of a creature that became extinct millions of years ago,' Amy chided.

'Oh, that. Yes, that was a little bit spaghetti western,' the Time Lord said, a boyish grin on his face. 'Well, it just so happens that it was the stegosaurs that brought me here. The poor beasts were obviously trying to return home.'

'Which is where, exactly?' Rory asked. 'Not here, surely?'

The Doctor smiled. 'Well yes, as it happens.'

CHAPTER EIGHTEEN
JUST ADD WATER

'So there are dinosaurs still living in the Florida Everglades at the end of the nineteenth century?' Rory exclaimed. 'Crikey! Who would've thought it?'

'No, not quite.'

'But you just said –'

'I said 'here', Rory,' the Doctor interrupted. 'Not 'now'.'

Rory stared at the Doctor. 'What?'

'As your good lady wife pointed out, the stegosaurs along with the rest of their kind became extinct millions of years ago. I should know; I was there – sort of. I mean, I had a hand in it, although

I should also point out that it wasn't my fault. Not entirely, anyway. Of course that hasn't stopped me from running into them in London during the Seventies and in caves under Wenley Moor in Derbyshire. But that's beside the point.'

'So what are you trying to say, Doctor?' Amy asked, trying to get him back on track.

'Okay, so once again for the hard of understanding, the stegosaurs were trying to return home, but their home is in the past. It was the fracture in time, located over this lake, that allowed them through from the Late Jurassic to the present. That is to say, the Florida Everglades towards the end of the nineteenth century.'

'The time fracture?' Rory said, mystified.

'Yes, well a time fracture,' the Doctor said. 'I told you the TARDIS detected a number of them on arriving here. I mean there's one that connects with the Cretaceous for a start. That's where the T-Rex really belongs and not in the Jurassic – whatever certain movie-makers would have you believe. But all of the time fractures are ultimately centred upon this lake – more precisely, this metal box. It's like the epicentre of an earthquake but with tremors and aftershocks rippling out in all directions. And the cracks don't all connect to the same place in time.'

Rory turned from the Doctor, who was busy with his sonic screwdriver again, to his wife. His eyes widened in surprise.

'Amy, your face,' he suddenly gasped.

'What? What is it?' Amy asked, putting a hand to her face. She knew she wasn't exactly looking her best. How could she, after being chased by dinosaurs and dunked in a river, and not to mention being thrown over a waterfall? But the concern in her husband's voice unsettled her.

'The cut on your cheek,' Rory spluttered.

'What? What about it?'

'It's... It's healing.'

'Well I should hope so too,' Amy said. 'It was stinging like nettle rash after we ended up in the river.'

'But it's not stinging now?' the Doctor asked,

scrutinizing her face as well now.

As it turned out, Amy realised, it wasn't.

'No,' she said. She tentatively ran her fingertips over her cheek, expecting the skin there to feel tender, only she couldn't feel anything. There was no scab; not even a raised welt. She probed harder, pushing at the firm flesh she found there. That didn't hurt either. 'What's going on?'

'The cut,' Rory said. 'It's gone. There's not a mark on you. It's like your cheek was never even cut in the first place!'

'Doctor?' Amy gave the Time Lord an anxious look. 'What's going on?'

'Oh, it's nothing to worry about,' the Doctor replied with a forced air of calm. 'Cellular regeneration is one of the less harmful side effects of the temporal energy leaking from the damaged time drive.'

When this comment clearly did nothing to relieve the anxious expressions on his friends' faces, the Doctor tried to clarify things for them.

'The time field the damaged drive's putting

out is causing your personal physical timelines to run backwards, repairing any recent damage and effectively restoring your youth. Although I wouldn't let your wife get too much closer, Mr Pond, otherwise you're going to find yourself married to the seven year-old Amelia Pond rather than the lovely twenty-something Amy.'

'And that's one of the less harmful side effects?' Rory said uncertainly.

'So how come it's not effecting you?' Amy asked, even as her husband dragged her away from the now humming metal cube.

'It is,' the Doctor confessed. 'But I've got a lot more youth to catch up on than you two.'

'So this is the source of the legend,' Amy said, realisation dawning on her now. 'This box is the Fountain of Youth.'

'In a manner of speaking, I suppose,' the Doctor agreed. 'The device must have lain here, at the heart of the Everglades, for hundreds of years. People came here, drank the waters of the lake because they were thirsty after all the effort of getting here, came within range of the damaged time drive, began to age in reverse, and had their youth was restored. Only they put it down to an effect of the waters, rather than the leaking time drive and – Voila! – one instant legend.'

'Just add water,' Amy said with a laugh.

'Ah yes, very good, Pond. Very good,' the Doctor said, grinning.

'So that's a time drive,' Rory said, pointing at the cube. 'That rusted old thing?'

'The trans-temporal drive from a vessel capable of time travel, to be precise.'

'Like the TARDIS you mean?' Amy said.

'Oh no, not like the TARDIS!' the Doctor laughed. 'The old girl might be a museum piece, but she's far more advanced than this primitive piece of junk.'

Amy's face suddenly lit up as she made the connection. 'But like whatever it was the TARDIS collided with whilst travelling through the Vortex!'

'Yes,' the Doctor said, flashing her an impressed smile. 'Just like that.'

CHAPTER NINETEEN
FLOTSAM AND JETSAM

The three companions were suddenly aware of another pair of eyes on them. It was the explorer, Sir Solomon Proudfoot. He was staring at them intently.

'I suppose it had to come out sooner or later,' the Doctor sighed theatrically, giving the gentleman explorer a cheery wave. 'Yes, we are in fact travellers in time and space,' he confessed, holding up his hands in mock surrender. 'Probably should have mentioned it earlier. But never mind, eh? A stitch in time and all that.'

'But Doctor, you just said that this thing has probably been lying here, hidden at the heart of the Everglades, for centuries,' Rory said, still trying to get his head round everything the Doctor had revealed in the last two minutes.

With one athletic spring, the Doctor jumped down from the top of the cube, landing up to his knees in muddy water.

'So I did, and so it has,' the Doctor said, 'judging by the level of corrosion and plant growth that was obscuring it when I first got here.'

'But the collision only happened this morning,' Rory persisted. 'And it's,' – he looked at the sky in confusion – 'dusk now? I think.'

'For us, it was only a matter of hours ago,' the Doctor explained, 'but you have to remember that travelling in time is never as simple as that. It comes with its own unique complications. Weddings and funerals are a nightmare for starters. Helps if you remember to attend them in the right order, of course.'

Rory stared at the Doctor in bewilderment.

'Would you care to explain?' Amy asked, backing up her husband.

'It's like this,' the Doctor began. 'We were

travelling backwards through time, heading for the Renaissance, when we collided with a ship that was travelling forwards through time. The force of the collision was enough to throw us forwards as well and almost cause the TARDIS to crash. Imagine if the other ship was badly damaged also – it's trans-temporal drive in particular – forcing the crew to jettison the device.'

'Ah, flotsam and jetsam,' Ishmael said knowingly.

Amy and Rory stared at the Doctor blankly. Proudfoot gave the Time Lord a suspicious look, his eyes narrowed.

'Imagine. The time drive emerges from the Vortex at this point in space several hundreds of years ago. A short time later, deprived of its time drive, the ship itself emerges from the Vortex and crash-lands somewhere nearby but – and this is the important bit – several hundred years later, in terms of how much time had passed here on Earth.'

'Then, last of all, the TARDIS lands on board the Venture, even further forward in time,' Amy said, understanding what the Doctor meant at last.

'And Bob – as they say – is your mother's brother,' the Doctor said triumphantly. 'Or, in my case, my grandmother's cousin seventeen times removed.'

Amy and Rory continued to gawp at the alien artefact. Ishmael was distractedly watching the flickering sky. Sir Solomon Proudfoot was watching the Doctor guardedly.

Amy became aware of a faint green light coming from within the peculiar device, escaping through the corroded time-worn cracks in its strange metal surface. Whatever the Doctor had been trying to do with his sonic screwdriver appeared to have had an effect.

'How do you know all this?' the explorer asked, his voice little more than a stupefied whisper.

'You wouldn't believe the things I've seen,' the Doctor said, a faraway look in his ancient eyes.

A thoughtful silence descended over those gathered in front of the damaged time drive.

It was broken abruptly by an eerie screech. It was a cry that echoed down through the aeons to the present. It was a sound with which Amy and Rory were already uncomfortably familiar.

'Oh no,' Amy breathed.

The Doctor perked up. The sound had caught his attention.

'Ah, now I'm guessing that would be your prehistoric pursuer,' the Time Lord said. A wary expression passed across his face like ripples across a lake.

Amy and Rory shot anxious glances all about them. There was no obvious cover, other than for the damaged drive. There were no convenient escape routes nearby either, as there had been the last time they had run into the T-Rex.

'I'm going to eat you,' the Doctor muttered. 'All of you.'

'I beg your pardon?' Amy exclaimed.

'I'm translating for you,' the Time Lord said. 'The dialect's Late Cretaceous, the accent is carnosaur . . . Too many teeth and a bucket-load of bad attitude?' The Doctor grinned. 'Yup, definitely a tyrannosaurus.'

CHAPTER TWENTY
TOO CLOSE
FOR COMFORT

'You got all that from just one roar?' Rory asked, secretly impressed.

'Well I did have a bit of help,' the Doctor confessed, 'since I can see it standing right over there.'

He pointed with his sonic screwdriver.

Amy and Rory snapped their heads round and gave a sharp intake of breath.

Ishmael clenched his mop-rifle all the more tightly.

It was little more than a sinister shadow at the edge of the morphing forest but its silhouette was unmistakeable. It loomed before the trees, its head swaying from side to side. Amy knew it must be sniffing the air. It was either still searching for them, or it had picked up the scent of the stegosaur herd again.

'Which way did you say your lift went?' Amy asked the Doctor.

'What, the stegosaurs?'

The Time Lord pointed behind him, towards the centre of the lake where the air shimmered as if with a heat-haze. One minute Amy could see clear blue skies above the lake. The next moment the skies were dark and a smoking volcano could be seen on the horizon.

'That way, back through the rift.'

Whether the T-Rex was following them or the stegosaur herd, it effectively made no difference.

'It's going to come this way,' she said.

'How can you be so sure?' the Doctor challenged her. 'It isn't going anywhere yet.'

The monster swung its head in their direction and set off towards them at a lumbering trot.

'Oh,' he said.

'I hate it when you're right, Amy,' Rory sighed. He turned to the Doctor. 'What do you reckon its top speed is?' he asked.

'Whatever it is you've got in mind, forget it,' the Doctor said. 'Forget it right now! Our best bet it to stay exactly where we are. Nobody make any sudden movements.'

Amy could feel the tremor of the terrible lizard's thudding footfalls as they sent ripples skittering away from the water's edge.

It was coming closer with every powerful stride. It was no longer just a dark shape before the tree line either. The tiger-stripe patterns covering its bronzed hide were clearly visible now.

'But Doctor it's still coming this way. It's getting closer!' Amy hissed.

'Yes, I know, thank you, Pond,' he hissed back. His attention was focused on his screwdriver now as he played with the sonic in his hands as if it was a Rubik's Cube.

The pitch of the humming coming from the time drive started to rise.

'So what are you going to do to stop it?' Rory demanded.

'Why me? Why is it always up to me?'

'Because you like it that way, Doctor,' Amy pointed out. 'So tell us – how are you going to get us out of this mess?'

Amy could hear the dinosaur's panting breath now as it quickened its pace. Either it could smell their fear or it was able to see the prey that had escaped it before quite clearly now.

'Well, Doctor?' Sir Solomon Proudfoot demanded, pulling his pistol from its holster.

The Doctor shot him a pained expression. 'Why's it always up to me? It's not my fault there's a fracture in time in the middle of the Everglades,' he returned, before adding under his breath, 'which makes a change.'

'Are you sure about that?' The explorer had obviously heard him.

The Doctor shot him a suspicious look.

'Very well then, Doctor, leave it to me,' Proudfoot said. He pointed his weapon at the rapidly approaching prehistoric monster.

'No!' the Doctor shouted, his eyes widening in horror as he laid eyes on the weapon. 'No guns. Put that thing away this instant!'

The explorer half-lowered the pistol. 'I take it this thing's a carnivore?' he said.

'Well yes, of course, I mean look at those teeth. They wouldn't be much good for grinding plants to a pulp now, would they? And then there's the position of its eyes on its skull. Good binocular vision. Just what a predator needs. But that's not the point,' the Doctor protested. 'Besides, a hand gun like that won't be any use against a T-Rex. A bullet from that thing wouldn't even penetrate its hide. You'd need something like an elephant gun at least.'

The nauseous stench of half-rotted meat washed over them as the Tyrannosaur exhaled a great gust of stinking air.

'That's all I needed to know,' Proudfoot growled.

Taking aim again, his finger tightened on the trigger, and he fired.

But there was no sudden, sharp bang. Instead a beam of intense red laser light burst from the muzzle of the pistol and streaked across the clearing, burning through the fetid air. It struck the T-Rex square in the middle of its skull.

A look of astonishment filled the tyrannosaur's beady yellow eyes as the blast fried its brain. But it took a moment longer for the creature's body to realise what had happened.

The dinosaur took another three lumbering strides towards them before its legs gave way beneath it. It crashed to the ground, sliding through the black mud of the lake shore towards them. It finally came to rest with its huge head only a few centimetres from the feet of an astonished Amy.

'Now that really was a little too close for comfort!' Amy gasped. Her whole body was shaking in shock.

The terrible lizard lay there, unmoving. Amy stared at the monster and it stared back at her. But there was no light in those eyes. The dinosaur was dead.

CHAPTER TWENTY-ONE
THE BIGGER PICTURE

The Doctor turned from the dead dinosaur to the Victorian gentlemen explorer. He looked at the man's seemingly ordinary, and yet clearly extraordinary, pistol.

'Where did you get that gun?' he asked in an appalled whisper.

'Doctor, can you repair the anomaly?' Proudfoot asked, avoiding the question.

'You had no right,' he fumed, his quiet voice full of menace. 'That was a magnificent beast, more worthy of life than –'

'The anomaly, Doctor,' Sir Solomon interrupted the Time Lord. 'Can you repair it?'

'You mean the time fracture that has been created by the damaged time drive, which is allowing dinosaurs to cross from the past into the present?'

'Can you?'

The Doctor regarded the explorer with narrowed eyes for a moment before giving his reply. 'Yes, I can.'

'Is nobody else here seeing the bigger picture?' Rory piped up.

The others turned to look at him. With everyone's attention on him he suddenly looked a little nervous but was determined to say his piece.

'Okay, we've got dinosaurs roaming the Florida Everglades, we've got a damaged time drive that's leaking timey-wimey stuff, or something, giving anyone who comes within range a free facelift, but what about the spaceship full of aliens that were forced to jettison the drive in the first place? Won't they be around here somewhere too, looking for it?' He glanced nervously at Proudfoot as he said this.

'Rory, you're a genius!' the Doctor suddenly exclaimed, grasping the young man by the arms and planting a smacker of a kiss on his forehead.

Amy grinned at the two of them. 'Well you didn't think I'd marry someone without at least half a brain, did you Doctor?'

'So the question we should be asking is, where is the other ship?' the Doctor went on, caught up in the conundrum now.

'Shouldn't the question be, why has this man got a laser gun?' Rory asked, still eyeing the explorer anxiously.

'No, no,' the Doctor said, dismissing Rory's concerns with a wave of his hand. 'I already know the answer to that.'

'You do?'

'Yes. Now, the ship has got to be somewhere close by. I mean it can't be that far away, either in space or time. After all, this' – he ran a hand over the corroded surface of the huge cube – 'is a rare treasure.'

The Doctor suddenly stopped, his brows

knitting and his expression darkening. Turning slowly from the cube, he fixed the explorer with a penetrating stare.

'Isn't that right, Sir Solomon?'

Amy and Rory both turned and stared at the explorer. Proudfoot stared back at them, his face grim. With a resigned sigh he put a hand to the copper-coloured bracelet clasped around his left wrist and gave it a twist.

Amy gave a gasp while Rory muttered something unrepeatable under his breath. Something was wrong with Proudfoot's face.

As Amy watched, unable to tear her eyes away from the man, she saw his features begin to warp and change. At first the distortion appeared as nothing more than a ripple across the skin of the man's cheek, as if he had been caught in the blast from a wind tunnel. But then the ripple spread across his whole face, distorting even his nose and forehead, that shouldn't have appeared as fluid as they did.

And as Amy continued to stare in horror at

the explorer, the warping effect became more pronounced, spreading out over his whole body. Ishmael gave a squeak of fear.

As Proudfoot's features changed, so did his height and build. He became taller and leaner. His skin became stretched tight across his skull. His clothes appeared to dissolve and evaporate revealing the body beneath, with both ribs and limb bones clearly defined.

Soon the Victorian gent resembled something that was little more than a seven-foot tale human skeleton covered with a thin layer of flesh, wearing a few scraps of what appeared to be leather and chainmail armour.

'Either he's an alien or he needs to see a doctor,' Rory gasped. The Doctor turned, one eyebrow arching. 'He's an alien, isn't he?'

'It certainly explains the laser pistol,' the Doctor replied. 'The question is,' he said, turning and looking up into the skeletal face of the looming creature, 'what manner of extraterrestrial are you?'

CHAPTER TWENTY-TWO
ONE IN A TRILLION

The creature looked down at the Time Lord through large eyes that looked like orbs of polished obsidian and blinked. Then it blinked again, with a second pair of eyelids positioned at right-angles to the first set.

Rory blinked back in startled response.

'From the look of you, I'm guessing Calibas,' the Doctor said, 'or at least a closely related species from within the vicinity of the Soronax Nebula. But the Calibas are scavengers.'

'Scavengers?' Amy echoed. She was aware of a ghastly whimpering sound coming from nearby. It was Ishmael. His face had gone a deathly white and Amy worried he might have a heart attack at any moment.

'The race is only capable of interstellar travel thanks to having nicked off with the warp engine from a Utraxan mining asteroid that crashed on their home-world, if I remember rightly,' the Doctor went on. He turned back to the looming alien. 'I'm guessing you 'borrowed' your perception filter tech from the Saturnynians or someone. You certainly shouldn't be in possession of a ship capable of time travel. Unless…'

Ishmael Cain had begun to babble. Amy shot him another anxious glance.

The old man looked terrified. He was backing away from the thing that had, until recently, been Sir Solomon Proudfoot, unable to tear his eyes off the alien. And he was still holding his mop-rifle protectively in front of him.

'Oh no, not them. Not them, not them, not them,' he gabbled.

'It's alright,' Amy said, taking a step towards the jabbering wretch.

'No, it's not!' he shrieked in return.

'Yes it is, the Doctor will sort it out,' – she turned back to the Doctor, adding – 'won't you, Doctor?' It wasn't so much a question as an instruction.

'So what are you?' the Doctor asked the skeletal creature again, drawing himself up to his full height and yet remaining a whole head shorter than the gaunt alien.

It blinked twice again before answering. 'We are the Calibas,' it said, in a voice that was underlined by a dry rattle.

'I knew it,' the Doctor said, a look of triumph on his face. Then his eyes narrowed. 'And we already know why you're here.'

The alien blinked twice.

'You're here for this,' the Time Lord said, tapping the time drive with his sonic screwdriver.

'We are only here because of you, Doctor,' the creature hissed.

'Now you can't blame that collision on me,' the Doctor snapped, suddenly defensive. 'That was a one in a trillion chance. We just got unlucky, that's all.'

'But you will help us,' the creature said.

The pistol gripped in its three-fingered hand had transformed in appearance too. It was now clearly a weapon of alien design, and it was being pointed at the Doctor.

'Yes, because you need my help, don't you? You didn't build this thing,' he said, tapping the time drive with his sonic again, 'and so you don't know how to fix it now that it's gone wrong. But I'm not going to help you if you're going to start waving that thing around.'

The Calibas double-blinked again, both its gaze and its gun still focused on the Time Lord.

'Anyway, what do you think I've been doing all along? And if you want me to keep on helping you you're going to have to put that thing away.' The Doctor stared pointedly at the alien weapon. 'I said no guns, didn't I? They're always more trouble than they're worth. Things always end badly when guns are involved.'

For a moment the Calibas didn't move. Then,

slowly, it put its pistol away in the holster hanging from the leather and chainmail skirt it wore.

'Thank you,' the Doctor said, and returned to running his humming sonic over the corroded cube. Deep inside the time drive, with every pass of the sonic screwdriver another broken link in its damaged circuitry was repaired.

The others waited in awkward silence as the Doctor grappled with repairing the damaged device. All except for Ishmael who was still whimpering unhappily to himself.

The Doctor broke off from his work, fixing the alien with a needling stare.

'You know what's really been niggling me?' he said. 'The time drive, your presence here, the dinosaurs… None of it explains this poor wretch's involvement in your little expedition into the Everglades.' The Time Lord nodded towards the petrified Ishmael. 'I mean, I take it you're not the only one of your kind stranded here?'

'You are quite correct, Doctor,' the alien confirmed. 'There is the rest of my crew.'

The old man started at that.

'It's alright,' Amy said, putting a comforting hand on his arm. 'He's not going to hurt you. No one's going to hurt you. It's going to be okay.'

'But Ishmael's clearly not one of you, is he?' the Doctor pressed, returning to work on the damaged device. The green glow coming from within the time drive was steadily increasing in intensity. 'So what's his part in all this? Why's he here?'

CHAPTER TWENTY-THREE
ON WINGS
OF FIRE

The Doctor suddenly stood bolt upright and slapped a hand to his forehead.

'Of course!' he exclaimed. 'How could I have been so stupid? Head's too full of stuff! I'm getting old and stupid!'

'What, Doctor?' Amy asked in nervous excitement. 'What is it?'

'You needed a psychic template to model your appearance on!' the Time Lord exclaimed, still addressing the alien.

'Like Prisoner Zero,' Amy gasped.

'Like Prisoner Zero,' the Doctor agreed.

'For us to create a believable false image our

cloaking technology requires it,' the Calibas explained.

'They came out of the storm!' Ishmael suddenly announced, a distant look entering the old man's eyes. 'On wings of fire and bringing death in their wake.'

'But that's not the only reason you've kept him around, is it?' the Doctor challenged.

'We found this one,' the alien said, indicating the cowering Ishmael with a nod of its head, 'floating amidst the wreckage of his ship after our own vessel crash-landed. After we had been forced to jettison the damaged time drive.'

'We set out from England months ago,' the old man went on, the same faraway look in his glassy eyes, 'in search of the Fountain of Youth.'

'The humans' vessel had clearly been wrecked during a storm,' the Calibas continued. 'He was the only survivor. We realised we would need to do something about our appearance to avoid discovery whilst we searched for the damaged drive. We scanned his mind and used what we found there –'

'Combined with your own particular brand of borrowed perception filter technology,' the Doctor interrupted.

'– to blend in better with our new surroundings.'

'So what you're saying is that you're all masquerading as dead men taken from the mind of a demented soul.'

'You might have been better off basing your look on One Million Years B.C., going with loincloths or something in fur,' Amy said, resting her weary legs by taking a seat on the muzzle of the dead dinosaur lying at the edge of the lake.

'Poor guy,' Rory said quietly, so that only the Doctor and his wife could hear. 'Must have driven him mad.'

'We don't know that,' the Doctor said. 'I think he might have been a bit that way inclined before the Calibas ever turned up, probably as a consequence of being a little bit psychic.'

'Can you be just a little bit psychic?' Rory asked.

'His latent psychic powers must have been given

a jump start by the opening of the time fracture,' the Doctor added.

'Really?' Amy said. 'You think he's psychic?'

'How do you think he knew so much about us and the TARDIS when we first turned up on board the Venture?' the Doctor said. 'I've seen it happen before plenty of times, such as back in Pompeii, in the lead up to Volcano Day. Ishmael's dormant abilities, combined with the fracture in time, made him sensitive to the currents of the Vortex. The side-effect of this was that he must have received glimpses of the past and future; other places as well as other times. It would have been a bit like watching a damaged film clip and discover bits and pieces about us without ever having met us before.

'Of course!' the Doctor suddenly announced, spinning on his heel in the muddy water. 'That's it!'

Rory and Amy looked at each other, open mouthed.

The Doctor turned back to face the Calibas. 'You were using poor old Ishmael here as a psychic compass!'

'A what?' Rory asked, flabbergasted.

'His sensitivity to the time fluctuations from the fractures allowed you to tell how close you were to the drive.

'You mean like whether they were getting hotter or colder?' Amy butted in.

'Precisely!'

The alien blinked twice.

'This one's sensitivity to the temporal disruptions allowed us to locate the unit when our other scanning instruments were unable to due to those very same disruptions.'

Amy scowled at the Calibas. 'Isn't that what I just said?'

Above them the sky continued to shift from clear blue, to the colour of congealed blood, to velvet black, and back again. All the while haunting cries echoed across the lake from an era lost in the mists of time.

'So where do we go from here?' Rory asked.

'Well if people would stop interrupting me,' the Doctor said grumpily, 'I might actually be able to finish fixing this thing.' He tapped the glowing cube with his sonic screwdriver again. 'Then we can think about sending the Calibas on their way again. And you can take your guns with you,' he said, addressing this last comment to the towering alien.

Ishmael was still shaking.

'Don't worry,' Amy said, getting up and putting an arm around the old man's shoulders. 'It's all right. I told you, no one's going to hurt you. You're not in danger anymore. You haven't done anything wrong.'

'Are you sure about that?' he said and pointed.

All eyes followed his quivering finger.

Beyond the corpse of the tyrannosaur, figures were emerging from out of the undergrowth. It was what was left of the crew of the Venture. But as Amy watched they began to morph and change. Arms and legs stretched and lengthened. Faces melted to become skull-like masks. Unable to help herself she gasped, putting a hand to her mouth.

The white, spectral shapes were moving towards

them now with long strides of their extended, bony limbs.

At least a dozen of the skeletal aliens were stalking towards the lake's edge and each one was holding a blaster. All of the weapons were trained on the Doctor and his human companions.

'Try telling them that,' Ishmael moaned.

CHAPTER TWENTY-FOUR
ZOMBIE DINOSAURS

'**H**old!' the alien's voice rang out loud across the lakeshore. Almost as one, the approaching skeletal stalkers stopped.

'Lower your weapons,' the creature formerly known as Sir Solomon Proudfoot instructed its kin. 'I have the situation under control.'

'Commander M'lek, you have found the time drive,' one of the closest of the approaching aliens declared. There was something like delight in the tone of its rattling voice.

'I have it Sol'n,' the Proudfoot-alien stated with pride.

A loud, reptilian screech sounded across the

mirror-smooth surface of the lake.

'Oh no, not again!' Rory complained. His gaze lingered on the T-Rex for a moment. It remained where it was, slumped in the mud and brackish water in front of the jettisoned drive.

'Look, it's very difficult to keep focused on what I'm supposed to be doing with these constant interruptions,' the Doctor grumbled, not once looking up from what he was doing, 'but don't worry, I'll have it fixed in another minute or two.'

Amy peered past the Doctor and the cube at the waters of the lake beyond. The sky above changed from black to purple in the blink of an eye and then she saw it. It hadn't been there a moment ago, but it was most certainly there now.

'Rory,' she hissed, pointing. 'Over there.'

Rory followed his wife's gaze. 'Marvellous,' he muttered. 'Is that what I think it is?'

'If you're thinking it's a triceratops then I think you're probably right,' Amy whispered back.

The aliens had seen the creature too.

'Calibas, prepare to defend the unit,' their leader

instructed them in its rattling desert-dry tones.

The other aliens responded immediately, targeting the dinosaur that was wading through the shallows of the lake towards them with their blasters. The lumbering beast raised its head and snorted, shaking its frilled collar and horns in anticipation of the battle that was surely to come.

His view of the approaching dinosaur blocked by the massive mechanism of the time drive, the Doctor glanced at the aliens.

'No!' the Doctor shouted. 'I said no guns! What's the matter with you lot? Which part of 'no' do you find so difficult to understand?'

His attention wholly on the aliens, the Time Lord suddenly realised that the Calibas weren't pointing their weapons at him or any of his companions. Curious as to what it was they were aiming at, he peered around the side of the corroded cube.

'Ah,' he said, catching sight of the charging bull triceratops for himself. 'Now I understand. But surely you're not going to shoot everything that comes through the rift, are you?' Pulling his head back in he turned to Commander M'lek. 'Now, I'm sure there a simple solution that doesn't involve you killing every living thing that comes through that time fracture.'

'Doctor, whatever it is you've got in mind,' Amy said anxiously, 'you'd better be quick.'

'Calibas, at my command,' M'lek instructed the others of his kind. Long alien fingers began to tighten on the firing mechanisms of twelve hyper-velocity laser blasters.

There was suddenly a tremendous splashing of water behind them as something massive struggled to its feet. Ishmael Cain screamed.

A bullish cry boomed across the disturbed lake. It was answered a moment later by a horribly familiar reptilian roar.

Calibas, Time Lord and humans turned as one from the snorting triceratops to face the resurrected tyrannosaur rising to its feet behind them. The carnivore stretched out its head and roared again.

'How…?' Rory began as he and Amy backed

away from the beast to join the Doctor. Ishmael just stood where he was, as white as a sheet, rooted to the spot by sheer terror.

'Of course!' the Doctor exclaimed. He sounded far more excited than seemed right, given the desperate nature of their situation.

'Of course, we're in trouble now?' Amy suggested. 'Of course, we're all going to die?'

'The leaking time field,' the Doctor said a manic gleam in his eye. 'It reverses the physical timeline of anyone – or anything – that's close enough to it! It healed your cut, it appears to be having a rejuvenating effect on old Ishmael and, as Proudfoot – or whatever he is – only just gunned it down, it's brought the T-Rex back to life.'

'Oh good,' Rory said. 'Just what we need. As if dinosaurs weren't bad enough, now we've got zombie dinosaurs.'

'No, not zombies,' the Doctor began. 'They're something else entirely.'

'Look, boys, fascinating as this is, don't you think we should do something more practical, like run?' Amy asked.

'I can't,' the Doctor said, 'I have to finish repairing the time drive otherwise this problem' – he pointed at the advancing T-Rex with his sonic – 'isn't going to go away.'

Amy stared up at the T-Rex and saw nothing but hatred in its eyes.

She could hear the Calibas shouting to each other in their rattlesnake voices but she could also hear the grunts and snorts of the enraged triceratops.

And then, giving another blood-curdling crocodile roar, the tyrannosaur started to run.

CHAPTER TWENTY-FIVE
A MILLION TIMES WORSE

They might have escaped the tyrannosaur's hungry wrath twice before, but Amy doubted they would escape it a third time.

And then she saw something in its jaundice-yellow stare that gave her hope. Its needling gaze wasn't focused on them but on something else beyond the cube.

But the alien commander clearly hadn't seen what she had seen. It was taking aim at the charging T-Rex with its blaster once again.

'No!' Amy shouted, flinging herself at the towering Calibas. 'Can't you see? It's not interested in us!'

She grabbed the alien's arm just as it squeezed the trigger, unbalancing it. The two of them fell into the swampy water with a splash. The alien weapon fired. A beam of red light shot from the muzzle of the gun and hit the cube, only a few feet from where the Doctor was still working on the device.

He gave a yelp of surprise and then rounded on the Calibas commander.

'I said no guns! Didn't anybody hear me? No guns! No guns, no guns – NO GUNS!' he shouted. 'They only ever make things worse. And, quite frankly, things were bad enough already!'

The gigantic carnivore thundered past the damaged time drive and the quaking humans. It ignored the gangly aliens too, as Amy knew it would, and instead headed straight for the centre of the lake. The triceratops was waiting for it there, stamping its feet and pawing the water. Its head down, the vicious prongs of its horns pointed forwards, it was ready to meet the ferocious charge of its age-old enemy.

'I told you we weren't in danger,' Amy said, fixing the alien with a furious scowl.

'Are you sure about that?' Rory asked, helping his wife up out of the lake. He was looking at the cube.

The glow emanating from within the device had changed from emerald green to a fiery orange, while the whirring hum it was generating was rising in pitch to a level that made Amy's ears ache.

'What's happening?' she said, looking at the Doctor. He was scanning the drive with his sonic screwdriver again.

'Our friend here's only made things about a million times worse,' the Doctor snapped. 'Him and his gun!'

And then he laid eyes on his companion again and his thunderous expression was replaced by a shocked 'O' of horrified surprise.

'Amy, I want you to step away from the time drive,' he said with the kind of forced calm that scared Amy more than a hungry T-Rex did.

'Why? What's the matter?'

There was something wrong with her voice. It sounded too high-pitched.

'What's going on, Doctor?' Rory asked, and Amy didn't like the worried tone in his voice either. The pitch was heightened in alarm. 'What's happening to her?'

'Hush!' the Doctor snapped. He was busy working on the cube again, looking more manic than ever.

'Never mind what's happening to me,' Amy replied. 'What's happening to you?'

Rory had always been slim but now he looked gangly, like he had as a teenager, when the two of them were growing up in Leadworth.

'Rory,' she gasped, 'you're getting thinner!'

The two days' growth of stubble he had collected on their latest adventure was gone too.

'I'm getting thinner?' he squeaked. 'What about you?'

Amy glanced down at herself. Her clothes were baggy about her and her boots were loose on her feet. Nothing fitted properly any more.

'I'm shrinking!' she squealed.

'You're not shrinking,' the Doctor butted in, without stopping what he was doing.

'Then what's happening to us, Doctor?' Rory pleaded.

The Time Lord turned and looked down at the two of them.

'You're getting younger,' he said. 'And at this rate, in a matter of minutes you'll be babies again. And after that...' The Doctor trailed off.

'After that what?' Amelia Pond demanded from within the swathes of Amy's Pond clothes that were now swamping her.

The Doctor took a deep breath. 'And after that... Well, you won't have existed at all.'

CHAPTER TWENTY-SIX
NO MORE TIME TO LOSE

'Right, there's no more time to lose,' the Doctor said, spinning on his heel and resuming his repair work on the time drive.

With a roar of hungry rage the tyrannosaur caught up with the triceratops at last. The three-horned beast grunted and braced itself, ready to meet the other monster's charge.

'Can't we just run away?' a youthful Rory asked. He looked about eight and appeared to have been dressing up in his dad's clothes.

'There isn't time for that. You've already lost about ten years each,' the Doctor said. 'Most likely more. And you don't want to stay stuck at seven years old, do you? Imagine. No more wine, and bedtimes back to 7.30.'

'Doctor. Look.'

The Doctor turned. It was Ishmael Cain who had spoken although he looked and sounded like a different man. He stood tall and strong now. Much of his grey hair had turned a lustrous black. The mad old nutcase had been replaced by a vigorous middle-aged man in his prime.

Only the Time Lord and the Calibas didn't look any different.

The Doctor followed Ishmael's sparkling gaze, turning his own eyes towards the flickering sky above. Only it wasn't flickering any more. It was now a permanent deep red, streaked with charcoal smudges of cloud and the volcano on the horizon had taken up permanent residence.

'What's going on, Doctor?' Amelia asked, fixing the Time Lord with her large hazel eyes.

'Are we in the past?' Rory asked. 'I mean dinosaur times?'

'No,' the Doctor said, hastily returning to his

work on the time drive. 'I mean, yes. And no.' He took a deep breath. 'What I mean is the time energy leaking from the cube is widening the fractures exponentially to the point where the present is effectively becoming the past. If I don't get the time drive repaired, and quickly, the dinosaurs will rule the Earth all over again and the human race will cease to exist. Again.'

'Yea, though I walk through the valley of the shadow of death,' Ishmael intoned, still staring at the scarlet sky, 'I will fear no evil.'

'Can you do it, Doctor?' Commander M'lek asked, something like fear shaping his alien features now. 'Can you repair the damage?'

'Yes,' the Doctor said through gritted teeth, 'of course I can. The actual question you should be asking is can I do it in time?'

CHAPTER TWENTY-SEVEN
ALL GOOD THINGS

The noise of the battling behemoths echoed across the lake but did nothing to drown out the high-pitched humming coming from the cube.

Unable to do anything else, Rory and Amy clasped hands, watching as the Doctor worked and the dinosaurs fought, anxious expressions on their young faces.

And then the ear-numbing noise began to drop rapidly in tone and the evil orange light coming from within the cube returned to a pulsing emerald green.

Amy could see the change in the cube for herself as well as hear it in the air around her. Now she could feel it too. Her whole body felt like it was stretching and swelling, and not in an unpleasant way either. Her muscles were tingling, like they did when she first woke in the morning and stretched.

She looked down at herself and watched as her legs became longer until her boots fitted once more, as did her clothes.

The same was happening to Rory. He was gaining in height before her very eyes, and as he grew to fill his own outfit, so the stubble appeared again on his face.

Unfortunately for him, Ishmael Cain was aging again as rapidly as the young couple. His muscles withered and his posture became stooped once more as his hair lost its colour in an instant.

'And – Voila! – Bob's your grandmother's cousin seventeen times removed!' the Doctor announced, waving his sonic screwdriver in a final flourish over his head before depressing a button on its side.

There was a sonic boom, like a clap of thunder, and a sudden change in air pressure. The force of it made Amy's eyes water, and she had to swallow hard to rid herself of the muffled sphere of silence that suddenly surrounded her.

In the blink of an eye the sky became a dusky blue-grey. The forest beyond the lake returned to normal and, like a video recording that had suddenly been turned off, the charging tyrannosaur and the snorting triceratops vanished.

Only the Doctor, his companions, the corroded metal cube, Ishmael Cain and the skeletal aliens remained.

'You did it, Doctor!' Rory exclaimed, somehow managing to look anxious and relieved at the same time. 'You really did it!'

'What did he do?' the old man asked.

'Fixed the time drive, of course.' The Time Lord flashed Ishmael Cain a child-like grin. 'And in doing so I also just happened to seal the time fractures. Nifty or what? There won't be any more dinosaurs sneaking back through from the prehistoric this way. The past's the past again and there's no time like the present.'

'And no more Fountain of Youth, I suppose,'

Amy said.

'All good things must come to an end,' the Doctor said sagely.

'Don't worry, I'm not complaining,' she replied. 'I'm not in a hurry to be seven again. Just imagine it. I'd have to take my GCSEs all over again! And they were bad enough the first time round.'

'So you will help us reattach the drive to our ship?' the Proudfoot-alien said, addressing the Doctor, its head bowed, its voice an emotionless rattle.

'You know a 'thank you' wouldn't go amiss,' the Doctor grunted. 'Not many people could do what I've just done, up to their ankles in stinking swamp water and armed with only a sonic screwdriver. Which I might add, is a tool intended for… tightening and loosening screws. I'm a bona fide genius, me!'

'Oh, come on, Doctor,' Amy said, nudging him in the ribs. 'You know that true geniuses are never really appreciated during their lifetime.'

'Tell me about it,' the Doctor said with a sigh.

'Try eleven lifetimes!'

'So you will help us reattach the drive to our ship?' Commander M'lek of the Calibas repeated.

'Yes, I'll help you,' the Doctor said, 'if only so I and my friends can get on with the rest of our day. Besides, I've had quite enough of you and your itchy trigger finger. You know, I was hoping to be catching up with Gutenberg by now and seeing how his Bible was going.'

The Doctor gave the cube one more hard stare. He looked like a car mechanic assessing a beat-up old banger. Amy half expected him to suck in a breath between his teeth at any moment and say, 'It'll cost ya.'

'What is it, Doctor?' she asked.

'I was just wondering how the Calibas are proposing to get this back to their ship, wherever it is,' the Doctor said. 'I don't know if it's possible to fly the ship here but I'm guessing not, otherwise surely you would have done that in the first place,' he went on, addressing the alien again. 'If that's not an option, which I suspect it isn't, if I could get back to the TARDIS I could rig up a tractor beam to tow the drive back to wherever the Calibas craft is parked.'

'It's alright, Doctor, we can solve that problem for ourselves,' M'lek rasped.

The alien turned to the rest of its crew. 'Calibas, to work.'

The Doctor, Amy and Rory moved back from the crashed cube. They took a seat on a mossy log, alongside the uneasy Ishmael, and watched as the spindly aliens surrounded the newly-repaired time drive.

Those who had been carrying packs on their backs ever since abandoning the Venture's lifeboats and continuing on foot, whilst still in human form, unslung them now. Putting the packs down on the ground, they proceeded to take out a number of metallic hemispheres. Each was as wide across as a dinner plate. The aliens then proceeded to attach them to every surface of the mud-splattered trans-temporal drive.

'I wonder who they borrowed those off,' the

Doctor muttered, so that only his companions could hear.

When all were in place, the Proudfoot-alien activated another device which it was holding in its spindly-fingered hands.

The air was suddenly alive with a throbbing hum and as Amy and the others watched the time drive rose gracefully into the air. Free of the clinging muck, it stopped. It remained hovering a metre above the surface of the lake, dripping mud and waterweeds.

The alien turned to face the astonished Time Lord and his companions. 'We are ready,' it said.

'No please,' the Doctor said, gesturing with an exaggerated flourish of his arm, 'after you.'

CHAPTER TWENTY-EIGHT
BUCKET OF BOLTS

Without packs of hungry or angry dinosaurs running fast and loose about the Everglades any longer, the walk back through the forest was much more straightforward – although the humidity didn't let up for a minute. Amy's clothes were still sticking to her skin and she constantly had to wipe the sweat from out of her eyes.

The Calibas had reactivated their cloaking devices although Amy wondered why, other than for the fact that it put Ishmael at his ease again. And perhaps that was good enough reason.

But there was no disguising the fact that they were trudging through the Everglades with a giant, four metre by four metre cube of alien design floating between them.

The route the Calibas took back through the forest was a long and meandering one. Amy, Rory, Ishmael and Sir Solomon Proudfoot's route to the lake had been much more direct, but then their journey had included a leap of faith off a hundred-metre tall cliff. That had been followed by a one-way ride downstream, over rapids and another waterfall, which wasn't really an option for the return journey.

They stopped as dusk gave way to night, now that the normal passage of time within the region had been restored. Amy fell asleep as soon as her head hit her rolled up bomber jacket pillow, despite the strange hoots, chirruping of insects and jabbering cries that assailed the forest as the sun set.

They set off again at dawn the next day. They reached the spot where the Venture's crew had beached their boats as the sun was climbing higher across the sky overhead.

Running the boats back out into the river and scrambling on-board, they let the current carry them back downstream. The time drive bobbed above the surface of the water as it kept up with the boats, being towed by the anti-gravitic device in Sir Solomon's hands. In no time at all, it seemed, the river returned them to the mangrove swamps bordering the coast and the sparkling waters of the Gulf of Mexico.

The sun was a beaten bronze disc now, its relentless heat pounding down upon their heads. The boats rode the swell of the choppy ocean waves, the curious expedition returning to the Venture at long last. A whole day had passed since they had set out on their quest to find the fabled Fountain of Youth.

Captain Bartholomew appeared pleased to see them. He also appeared completely unfazed by the fact that Proudfoot's party had brought an alien trans-temporal drive unit back with them from their mission into the Florida Everglades. He did appear slightly more perturbed by the fact that the crew were somewhat depleted since he had said last seen them.

'So you're one of them too,' the Doctor said, clambering up the rusted boarding ladder onto the deck of the tramp steamer.

The captain looked at him for a moment, brows knitting and eyes narrowing in suspicion.

'If by 'one of them' you mean –'

'The Calibas. You're one of the Calibas,' the Doctor interrupted.

'Then yes. I'm 'one of them'.'

The Doctor's companions joined him back on-board the ship, as did Ishmael Cain and the rest of Proudfoot's expeditionary party. The sailors quickly set about lowering the time drive into the hold on its anti-grav repulsors.

'Right, well let's not beat about the bush any longer,' the Time Lord said. 'If you'd like to take me back to your ship then we can get this thing reattached' – he waved his screwdriver at the descending cube – 'and, more importantly, we can send you on your way. I'm sure you could do with my help.'

'But we're already there,' Proudfoot said, a wry smile curling the lips of his strangely human face.

'What? Oh, I see. At the bottom of the sea, is it?' the Doctor said. He peered over the side of the ship as if half-expecting to see an alien craft suspended there in the greeny gloom below the waves. 'Can't be helped really. After all, only one third of the Earth's surface is actually land so the statistical probability is that you're always more likely to end up in the drink.'

'No, Doctor,' the cloaked alien said, still smiling. 'You don't understand. The Venture is our ship.'

'What?' Rory gasped, staring at the rolling ship. 'This old bucket of bolts is your ship?'

'Why not,' Amy said. 'We fly around the universe inside a 1950s police box.'

'Good point.'

'So your ship utilises the same cloaking technology that gives you a human appearance, all based on the memories of poor Ishmael here,' the Doctor said.

'That's right, Doctor,' Proudfoot confirmed.

'Right then. Well you'd better show me where you want your reconditioned time drive installed.'

A croaking guttural roar – that spoke of a primeval hunger that could not be satisfied – cut through the splash of the surf and the distant cries of sea birds.

'Don't tell me...' Amy began.

Rory looked at her with terror in his eyes. 'The liopleurodon!' he finished.

CHAPTER TWENTY-NINE
DAMAGE LIMITATION

'But Doctor, I thought you sealed the time fractures when you repaired the drive,' Amy said, struggling to hide the anxiety from her voice.

The roar sounded over the waves again, closer this time.

'I did!' the Doctor protested.

The Venture suddenly lurched. All on-board were sent staggering towards the starboard bow, as something struck the ship a resounding blow from below. Amy gave a scream despite herself.

The Doctor's face fell. 'Only trouble is, in doing so I also trapped whatever had already come through the rifts here, in the late nineteenth century.'

'Now he tells us.'

The sea beside the ship suddenly exploded. A great drenching wave crashed across the deck, and all those on it, as a monstrous, reptilian head broke the surface, jaws agape, eyes glistening like black pearls, and with murder on its mind.

The Doctor grimaced in embarrassment. 'I forgot about the liopleurodon.'

'The T-Rex went back through,' Amy said as she began to piece the puzzle together for herself.

'And the stegosaur herd had already gone back through,' the Doctor continued.

'The triceratops never made it through in the first place,' Amy added.

'Which just leaves the liopleurodon.'

The croaking reptilian cry echoed eerily over the ocean.

'I hope.'

For a moment Amy could have believed that it was they who were trapped in the primeval past and not the super-predator that was trapped in the present. Although it wasn't the present as she knew it – it was still the late nineteenth century.

'I've stranded it here,' the Doctor said, his voice quiet. 'I'm such an idiot!' he suddenly shouted, smacking his forehead with the palm of his hand. 'How could I have been so careless?'

'But it wasn't your fault,' Amy said, grabbing hold of the gunwale as another wave swamped the deck.

'The damage was already done, Doctor,' Rory added.

'Right, well I think it's time for a little damage limitation then, don't you?' the Doctor said, his expression grim.

'Come on!' he called to the leader of the aliens who was still masquerading as the late Sir Solomon Proudfoot. The Doctor bounded across the deck with the surefootedness of a cat. 'Let's get the drive reinstalled and then get you out of here.'

'What about the beast?' the alien who had taken on the form of Captain Bartholomew demanded.

'You'll just have to do your best to fend it off!' the Doctor called back. 'But no guns!' he added sternly, before disappearing through a hatch that led down into the belly of the steamer-cum-alien-time-ship. He was followed by the Proudfoot-alien.

'But you said yourself, Doctor,' the captain called back, 'it shouldn't even be here!'

'I won't have the creature's death on my conscience along with the knowledge that it's been displaced time. If you kill it, I'll leave you stranded here too!'

'Do as he says!' Proudfoot shouted back.

The captain studied the sea beyond the bow of the boat where the liopleurodon had dived beneath the waves again. 'You heard him!' he ordered the crew. 'Grab anything you can and keep the beast at bay, or none of us will be leaving this time-forsaken planet!'

CHAPTER THIRTY
A SECOND CHANCE

The crew, with Rory and Amy's assistance, battled the marine monster for a good ten minutes, although it seemed considerably longer. The liopleurodon kept coming back for another go. Here an oar turned to matchwood between its crushing jaws; there a recovered lifeboat was knocked from its cradle. The monster continued to slam its massive body into the side of the steamer, sending all those on deck reeling and struggling to stay on their feet.

'Done?' Amy asked as the Doctor emerged from the hatch ten minutes later. His hair was still not dry from his soaking on deck, but he looked better than either she or Rory did.

'Done!' he announced proudly.

'So, we can go now?' Rory asked, wielding the paddle of a lifeboat in defence of the ship as if it were a battle-axe.

'Absolutely,' the Doctor said, with a heart-felt sigh of relief.

The three time travellers turned from the gunwales and the battle with the beast. Ducking and weaving across the deck, and along the narrow gangways, they made for the stern of the ship.

There, parked between piles of tarpaulin-draped crates, was what appeared to be a weathered wooden box. At some stage in its life it had been painted blue. A broad smile spread across the Doctor's face as he caught sight of the TARDIS again.

'Hello, old girl,' he said, patting the door of the police box affectionately. 'Missed me?'

Using what looked like an ordinary house key, he unlocked the TARDIS and ushered his friends inside.

Amy's face lit up in excitement as she trotted inside after her husband. And then suddenly she halted. 'What about Ishmael?' she said.

'Good point!' the Doctor exclaimed. 'I knew I'd forgotten something.'

Amy laughed. 'You know, for someone with a brain the size of a planet, you can be really stupid sometimes.'

'Right, don't go anywhere. I'll be back in a tick!' With that the Doctor disappeared again.

He dashed back across the deck, dodging the mini tsunamis that the liopleurodon's thrashing flippers sent crashing over the bedraggled crew. He found the old man, his mop still clasped tightly in his hands, standing shoulder-to-shoulder with Sir Solomon Proudfoot, and beating the monster on the snout whenever it came within reach.

'Ishmael!' the Doctor gasped. 'Come with us!'

The old man looked back at the Doctor. His eyes sparkled under the brim of his pith helmet. 'Go where, sah?'

The Doctor ducked a swipe from the sea

monster's forelimb. 'From here!' He had to shout to be heard over the croaking cries of the beast and the crash of water against the steel hull of the ship.

'In that flying blue box of yours, you mean?'

'That's the one.'

The Doctor was suddenly aware of a throbbing bass note, that he could feel as much as hear. It rose from the bowels of the ship, reverberating through every fibre of his being.

'Thanks for thinking of me,' the old man said. A tear was forming at the corner of one eye. 'But I'm alright now. The visions that tormented me for so long have gone, now that the fractures have closed. And besides, I'm back amongst my old crew,' he added. 'I'd rather stay, if it's all the same to you.' He directed this last comment at the thing that now resembled Sir Solomon Proudfoot once more.

'You would be most welcome, Ishmael Cain,' Proudfoot replied.

'If you're sure?' the Doctor pressed.

'I'm old, Doctor. I'm lucky to be alive at all after the hurricane wrecked the Venture and drowned its crew. Not many people get a second chance at my time of life. But I have a feeling that the real adventure is only just beginning.'

'Never let it be said that I would ever stand in the way of a man and his destiny,' the Doctor announced. Suddenly standing to attention, he saluted smartly. 'Ishmael, it's been a pleasure, sah!'

'Likewise, Doctor,' the old man said, returning the salute.

'Sir Solomon, or Commander M'lek, or whatever it is you're called,' the Doctor mumbled, nodding at the alien currently wearing the form of a Victorian gentleman explorer.

'Doctor,' Sir Solomon Proudfoot returned. 'And, as I believe this body would say, thank you.'

CHAPTER THIRTY-ONE
LIFE'S LITTLE MYSTERIES

'Right,' the Doctor announced, flinging himself through the door and into the TARDIS's main console chamber. The lock caught with a click as he slammed it securely shut behind him. 'Time we were off!'

Amy and Rory were already waiting in eager anticipation beside the hexagonal control console, ready to go.

The Doctor joined them there, deftly flicked a few switches, pulled a few levers and wound a few handles. In response, the time rotor began to rise and fall as the TARDIS's engines wheezed into life. There was a jolt and then stability returned.

Pulling down the viewing monitor, the Doctor turned a knurled knob and an image flickered into being on the screen washed with grainy static.

'It's the Venture,' Rory said as the image of the ship resolved into clarity on the screen. 'Does that mean we're not on-board anymore?'

'Not anymore,' the Doctor said. 'Now watch this.'

They watched as the Venture became suffused with lurid green light. They could see the liopleurodon too, although it was retreating now, repelled no doubt by the eerie emerald glow, as any animal would have been. And then the creature abruptly dived from view beneath the waves.

Rory's jaw dropped even lower as the tramp steamer began to rise into the air. When it was several metres above the churning surface of the ocean it stopped, hovering over the turmoil left in its wake, as sea water ran in torrents from its deck and hull.

The glow intensified until the screen was ablaze with searing white light. A moment later, the light vanished, accompanied by a sound like the pop of changing air pressures. Blinking in the aftermath of the brilliant glare, Amy stared at the screen, her face washed in the orange-green glow of the console room.

All that she could see through the viewer was the surge of the sea, and nothing more. 'It's gone,' she said.

'Thank goodness for that,' the Doctor said. 'My quick fix worked.'

'So the Calibas are on their way again, travelling through time,' Rory said.

'Yes, but back to their own time. I took the precaution of locking the time drive temporal destination coordinates. Don't want any more near misses, do we? And we should be on our way too.' The Doctor turned his attention to the console controls once more. 'What did we agree on in the end?'

'What about the liopleurodon?' Amy asked, still staring at the empty ocean as seen via the TARDIS viewer. 'I mean it's still stuck out there somewhere, isn't it, all alone, a hundred million years from home?'

'Never mind that,' Rory said. 'There's a prehistoric marine predator roaming the oceans of late nineteenth century Earth.'

'And your point is?' the Doctor asked.

'How are people going to explain that away?'

'Perhaps they won't,' the Doctor said. 'It will just have to remain one of life's little mysteries. And where would be the fun in life if it weren't for the odd mystery here and there?'

'Like the Loch Ness Monster, you mean?' Rory said.

'Something like that,' the Doctor replied. 'Now, where were we? I don't know about you, but after all that I fancy visiting somewhere nice and quiet – like the Hundred Years War!'

And with that, wheezing like an asthmatic elephant as it rotated slowly above the waves of the Gulf of Mexico, the blue wooden box dematerialized.

THE END

DOCTOR DW WHO

HORROR OF THE SPACE SNAKES

GARY RUSSELL

CHAPTER 1
TRAVELLING MAN

The Doctor was in the TARDIS, standing in front of a tall mirror. He was gently swaying from side to side swishing his new long green overcoat around.

'Good fit, yes?'

No response.

Of course not – the TARDIS was empty.

Amy and Rory were safely tucked up in their new home in 21st century Leadworth. He tried to picture Amy, out in the back garden, probably battling with a barbeque while Rory was off somewhere, perhaps whizzing around the Forest of Dean in that new sports car the Doctor had got him.

And River Song? Back in her cell at the Stormcage Facility in the 51st century, most likely. Unless it was night time, in which case she and a younger version of him (or maybe a slightly older one, who knows) were probably out somewhere, dining in Paris, examining modern art in New York or painting the town a variety of shades of *rood* in Amsterdam.

Or perhaps they were in Cersis Major, climbing the golden rock faces. Or Talusia, helping the Weavers and their web-sky-cities stay aloft.

Or maybe even having a swift bottle of pop with Jim the Fish and his extraordinary family under the starlight on his waterworld.

And he didn't want to think what the dozens of other fellow travellers he'd known and befriended over the years were up to since leaving his TARDIS. Because that way, madness lay.

But no matter what face he wore, the Doctor never liked being alone in the TARDIS.

The TARDIS, he was convinced, disliked it

equally. Somehow everything seemed a bit more sluggish, a bit slower to respond. The lights seemed a bit dimmer, the ambient temperature a few degrees cooler.

'I know,' he said to the time rotor as it rose and fell within its glass tubing. He stroked a few of the controls on the console, and blew some dust off the old record player that he'd restored after someone chucked a spear into it once.

He couldn't remember how or why or when that happened. Things like that tended to blur in his memory. Having companions aboard the TARDIS always kept things in focus; if someone had been here, he'd have been able to say the exact date and time that it had happened, he'd have a point of reference for it, something to trigger the memory.

'Doctor,' he declared aloud to himself. 'Doctor, Doctor, Doctor, someone is getting a bit maudlin, and a teensy weensy bit stir crazy. Loneliness is all in the mind – there's a universe or ten out there to explore. Tell you what Doctor, let's play "Reckless

Randomiser" – that's always fun.'

He threw himself at the coordinate control panel, and shut his eyes, simultaneously rolling the palms of his hands over all the switches, dials, touch-sensitive rollers and archaic levers and pulleys, all at once.

And then he'd count to ten, turn around four times and see where he was heading next.

"Reckless Randomiser" could be such fun.

He did this.

And looked at the result.

'Typical.'

He pulled a switch and on the huge TARDIS scanner, and all the smaller screens dotted around the control room, a planet appeared.

'Earth. What's random about that? Or reckless, to be honest?'

The Doctor felt a twinge in his head. 'Oww. Ow, ow and oww again,' he said, diving into an inside pocket of his long green coat and pulling out the little wallet containing his psychic paper.

He stared at it.

HELLO THERE. NEED HELP PLEASE. UNIT MOONBASE ONE. ARCHITECTS (AND BUDGET) GETTING OUT OF HAND. NEED SORTING BY THE MINISTRY. THANX. THE KOMMANDANT.

He thought about it. UNIT – yup knew them, not always fond of them but there had been a few golden moments. The Moon, yup, that he knew. Been there more than once – indeed, he'd been to Moonbase One itself a few times over the centuries, where it had been used variously as everything from a weather control system to a prison to a huge children's amusement park. Oh, that rollercoaster...

The Kommandant? That, however, meant nothing, no one he knew.

Occasionally, the psychic paper picked up messages not actually meant for him, sort of like picking up a satellite TV station from another country when retuning the digibox.

Or at least that was how Rory had described it once. The Doctor had agreed in principle even if he didn't quite get the analogy.

And this absolutely looked like one of those times. After all, what did he know about architects? There was something about Shadow Architects in his memory but he was pretty sure that wasn't the same thing at all...

The TARDIS landed.

The Doctor threw a look up into the ether. 'Thank you. Are you trying to tell me I need something to occupy myself with? Well, all right. We'll nose around for half an hour – just thirty minutes. Then I'm coming back and we'll find somewhere really random to go that you can't influence.'

As if in answer, the TARDIS lights went a bit brighter.

With a sigh, the Doctor checked his psychic paper was back in his trousers, that there was a Jammie Dodger in his top pocket and a smile on his face and he exited the TARDIS.

And walked straight into a door. The TARDIS had deposited him inside a very small storeroom. *Very* small.

He reached out and found a wheel on the door, and turned it with one hand, which was strangely difficult. It was designed for two-handed turning, but as his right hand and arm were squashed between the TARDIS and the wall, that was not going to happen.

The door eventually swung open (outwards, into the corridor, luckily) and the Doctor heaved himself into the brightly lit space. Bland walls, bland floors and bland ceilings. Everything was varying shades of dull white. In other words, bland.

'Imagine if this place had colour,' he muttered. 'Some pictures pinned up. Or some nice murals painted on the walls. Now that would be nice.'

Everything was built on a curve, so he couldn't see what was, literally, just around the corner.

Popping the Jammie Dodger in his mouth, he walked forward, keeping a hand close to the psychic paper in case it was needed. Every so often he passed a UNIT insignia stencilled on a door, and military-types were often shoot first, ask questions afterwards types.

As he munched on his biscuit, two men in UNIT black coveralls and red berets marched towards him. 'Here we go...' he muttered under his breath.

'Oh there you are,' smiled one of the soldiers, 'we thought you'd got lost.'

The other tapped his ear, activating some kind of bluetooth device. 'Greyhound Eighteen to Trap Six, we found him, Kommandant.'

'Wasn't aware I was lost,' the Doctor smiled. 'My name is –'

'S'alright, Mr Moss,' the first soldier said. 'People take a wrong turn up here and it can take you an hour just to walk the circumference of the Base. Not a problem. The others are waiting for you. This way.'

With a shrug to himself, the Doctor let himself be marched along the curved Moonbase corridor, noting various rooms and signs that he passed. One in particular intrigued him.

'What's HEART?' he asked.

'All will be explained by the American,' a soldier

said.

'Ah, Americans, they know everything,' the Doctor joked. 'Or think they do.'

'That's right sir,' said the soldier in a tone of voice that neither implied he agreed or didn't.

As they walked on, a door opened behind them.

'Sergeant?'

The two soldiers and the Doctor stopped and turned. Both UNIT men saluted.

'Mr Moss, yes?' continued the man in a German accent. He was looking at the Doctor, clearly thinking *he* was this Mr Moss person. 'I am the Kommandant. May I say I am very glad to have you up here.'

'My pleasure, Kommandant,' the Doctor said. 'Your message sounded... urgent. I got here as fast as possible. Your lads here were marvellous at finding me too. I got lost, I'm afraid.'

The Kommandant looked the Doctor up and down.

Sensing a challenge to his sartorial elegance, the Doctor flicked his hair back a bit and tweaked his bow tie.

But the Kommandant smiled, perhaps used to such... eccentricity in the civilians that came to the Moon every so often. 'Listen, if you can sort out Mr Galan, I'll be incredibly grateful. See what you think and after your meeting, let's talk again. Sergeant Tanner?'

'Yes sir?'

'Stay with the architects please and bring Mr Moss back to my office afterwards, would you?'

'Sir.'

Sergeant Tanner and the other soldier escorted the Doctor on again. It occurred to the Doctor to wonder what he would do when the real Mr Moss – who they clearly believed him to be – wandered up from wherever he was. But he'd cross that bridge when he came to it.

A few minutes later, he was being ushered into a huge room, with a high domed ceiling, and kitted out with foldaway chairs arranged in a circle around the outside. Many of the chairs were occupied, although not so many that the people outnumbered them.

In the centre of the room was a relief map of the Moon's surface, with the Moonbase at one side.

Standing by this map, addressing the seated listeners, a mixture of civilians and UNIT personnel of differing ranks, was a tall man in glasses.

Beside him, a shorter man was relentlessly tapping on a tablet, swiping pages away and doing that strange finger movement that meant he was enlarging or decreasing images now and again.

They hadn't yet invented a proper word for that. They would. The Doctor thought "zooping" was a good word for it – mainly because in three hundred years time, he'd accidentally added "zooping" to the Galactic Humanish Dictionary without giving it a definition. This seemed as good a time as any to come up with one.

The man continued "zooping" and the taller one continued talking.

Both were American, both had dull voices that made the Doctor sleepy and both were talking a load of nonsense about the surface of the moon, mapping its peaks and troughs and something about buying the dark side back from the Korean Unity, although no one knew how they owned it in the first place.

'Oh, that was me...' the Doctor was about to say, remembering the game of draughts he'd won against Kim someone or other back in the 1950s, which had meant that in seventy years, the two Koreas would amicably become one, and, in exchange, they'd get real estate on the moon. Or something. The Doctor had never been too sure of the details as River Song had been there, causing trouble with one of the more pompous families and they'd had to make a quick getaway.

So here, in the assembly area of Moonbase One, the Doctor thought it best to keep that one to himself.

He was aware that standing by the door, getting slightly in the way of Sergeant Tanner and other guards, was a small man in white coveralls, carrying a red toolbox. He seemed to be a maintenance man, trying to fix a problem with one of the air vents at the point where the wall met the floor.

He watched the man unscrew the small vent, but couldn't quite see what else he was doing. To the Doctor it seemed that all he was doing was staring into the vent, before replacing the grill, nodding to the soldiers and then leaving. The whole exercise seemed to have been a waste of time. Oh well.

'Bob?' called out one of the American voices. 'Bob?' it repeated.

After a second the Doctor realised that the two Americans were looking at him.

'You're Bob Moss, yeah?' the taller one asked loudly.

'Yes. Yes, absolutely. Bob Moss. Ministry of... Architects and Cartographers,' he said with a smile. 'Sorry I'm late.'

The Americans looked like they'd never heard of such a Ministry (hardly surprising).

'Zeppatelli,' the tall one said, 'take Bob outside, show him the lay of the land.'

The smaller man nodded and wandered over to the Doctor, holding out a hand to shake, which the

Doctor did.

'C'mon, Bob,' Zeppatelli said. 'Galan can talk for hours, and we don't need to listen to his plans for the other Moonbases. I guess you've read the specs and schedules by now.'

'Oh yes. Absolutely,' lied the Doctor. 'Nice to meet you after... so long.'

Zeppatelli frowned. 'Heck, it's only been three weeks since you emailed us.'

'Feels like forever,' the Doctor said quickly.

Zeppatelli shrugged.

They headed back out of the big room, but the Doctor stopped and eased Sergeant Tanner to one side very slightly and peered down at where the maintenance man had unscrewed the vent cover then put it back.

Nothing.

Nothing weird. Or strange. Or unusual. Nothing except the fact that he had done it at all. Perhaps, the Doctor decided, that was mysterious enough.

Sergeant Tanner told them he'd lead them to

the Suit Room to get kitted up for a Moonwalk. And that he was coming with them.

A few moments later, they were seated in a small buggy, and Zeppatelli was driving it out across the dusty surface – a bit too fast for the Doctor's liking.

CHAPTER 2
NEW SUNSHINE MORNING

26 June 2017

Lukas Minski watched as the door swung outwards, slowly but steadily.

His heart felt like it was going ten to the dozen as he stepped through the doorway – it was his first time, and he was determined to enjoy it, fear and everything.

Because what he was doing was dangerous. No two ways about that. Each step was potentially lethal – a misstep here, a trip there, anything could kill him.

There were more things that could kill him in

a square metre than could save him – something drilled into him from the earliest days in training. Not a nice thought, but one that he'd never forgotten. After all, no one wanted a repeat of what had happened to Carlos.

As he took a few steps forward, he could see the buggy parked ahead, and a group of three guys standing around, waiting for him.

In his hand, he carried his red toolbox – everything he needed to justify what he was doing was in there.

He eventually made it to the buggy and could see straight away what the problem was – one of the wheels had hit a rock and twisted, shearing the rear axel.

'That's a big job,' he explained to the guys.

'Really? I hadn't noticed,' said the American. The driver, Lukas knew. Arrogant man, but good at his job. He was an architect and was responsible for what were currently referred to as "the lower levels", usually said in a tone of voice that suggested they were somehow scary and threatening. They weren't. They were exactly what they said – lower levels. Architects always liked to exaggerate their own importance.

'What speed were you to be doing?'

'Who cares,' said one of the others. That was the UNIT man – he wore sergeant stripes on the arm of his spacesuit. Lukas tried to remember his name without success. 'Can you fix it?'

'Yes sir, but it is taking me up to maybe a couple of hours - I'm new to this. You as well to go back in and wait, yes?'

The three men looked in Lukas' direction – he could tell from their limited body language that they weren't happy, but there was nothing that could be done. If they'd driven the buggy less recklessly, they wouldn't have this problem, would they?

Three of them walked off immediately, but one hung back.

'You going to be all right out here alone?' he asked Lukas in an English accent. 'Your first week, yeah?'

Lukas said he'd be fine, and held his toolbox up carefully. 'My first job actually out here,' he said proudly. 'This toolbox, it was a gift from Darya, my wife. New tools for a new career.'

'New career, Mr...?'

'Minski. Lukas Minski.' Lukas said. 'I work in the UNIT museums, in Georgia, lots of treasures and pictures. Very pretty, but often sad stories. The museum, it was full of things that it shouldn't have, things not originally theirs,' he said. Then he coughed, as if realising he was rambling on too much. 'But I grow bored, sat all day, watching fat, rich people stare at things they not understand. I like using my hands, so Darya say it was time to do something new before I go mad with the boredom.' He laughed. 'Never argue with the wife, yes?'

The Englishman nodded. 'Absolutely. I've tried arguing with mine, all that ended up doing was changing the entire history of the universe. More than once I imagine.'

Lukas stared at the man, but couldn't see his

face through the visor. 'Okay,' he said a little carefully, as if talking to a madman. 'So now I am working with my hands, mending things, making everything from the lights work to fixing the cars. I believe you English say I get to the heart of the matter, no?'

The Englishman laughed. 'I'm not really English, Lukas. I just do the accent.'

Again Lukas, unable to see the man's face, couldn't be sure how serious he was being. He bent down and tapped a six-digit code on the red toolbox's lock and it sprang open.

'Security,' he said. 'Have to keep my tools safe, yes?'

The Englishman was watching Lukas intently – he could feel his eyes on him even through the darkened visor. 'Absolutely,' he said. Then he pointed to a photo glued into the underside of the now-open lid. It showed a blonde woman and a small blonde girl. Very austere, standing in front of a church, dressed in black.

'Family?' he asked Lukas.

Lukas glanced down at the photo. 'It is to be the day of Anni's birth next week. She is to be ten. She was expecting to have a big party, but I don't think so now. That is making me sad. She is the reason for everything I am doing.'

Lukas was still getting his tools ready when it occurred to him the Englishman had stopped speaking. He glanced up, and the Englishman seemed to be staring across the path where the buggy had stopped, his hand raised trying to keep the sun off his polarised visor.

'What is problem?' Lukas asked him.

'Dunno,' the Englishman said. 'Thought I saw movement.'

Lukas stood up. 'What kind of movement? No one else scheduled to be around here, are they?'

'No, it wasn't people. It was like… oh well, doesn't matter.'

Lukas frowned. 'Seriously, what is the problem?'

The Englishman shrugged. 'You'll think I'm mad.'

'You work here,' Lukas laughed. 'Of course

you are mad. We all are to be up here.'

But the Englishman wasn't laughing. 'You know that movement you see in those nature documentaries – those snakes that move sideways in a sort of S shape?' He made the movement with his gloved space suited hands.

Lukas laughed. 'You see snakes out here? Sidewinders? Here?'

The Englishman put his hands up in mock surrender. 'Yeah, okay. Must be the sunlight creating mirages or something. Anyway, I'll see you inside. I'll get Zeppatelli to buy you a drink to say thanks for fixing the buggy he's wrecked.'

Lukas smiled. 'Okay, yes, deal. I find you in the Mess in ninety minutes or so.'

The Englishman tapped the side of his head with his finger in mock salute. 'Cheers, Lukas. See you later.'

Lukas watched him wander back to join his friends inside and as the door closed behind him, shutting him away from Lukas, the mechanic was pleased. He preferred working alone and in silence.

He loved his machines, loved fixing them.

He had been building a small model of a buggy to celebrate his daughter's birthday. He knew it wasn't an ideal use of his free time, but shopping was… limited here, so homemade presents were the best you could get.

As he bent down to his toolbox, Lukas's eyes drifted towards where the Englishman had seen the strange movement.

And for a second Lukas saw something too. Perhaps it was a trick of the sunlight on the ground.

He started to focus on repairing the knackered buggy axel.

And then he stopped again. Something was there, he just knew it.

The trouble with spacesuits and their visored helmets was that they limited your vision – Lukas could look straight ahead and a bit to either side, but by the time he'd moved his entire body around in zero gravity, whatever was behind him could have leapt up and grabbed him.

Nevertheless, he did turn around – and there

they were.

Facing him. Thin, silvery creatures.

They were snakes, like cobras from Earth, with the hoods. Dark sulphurous yellow eyes that suggested decay glinted, eyelids nictitated back and forth as they seemed to focus in on him.

Their hooded heads rocked back and forth and one of them opened its mouth to reveal sharp fangs.

But what was really freaky... other than the simple fact there were creatures, *snakes* even, on the Moon's surface, was that they were metallic silver rather than the multi-coloured scales of snakes back home. Maybe it was the sunlight, maybe it was madness, but Lukas swore there was something about their skin... not robotic, more like – but no, that was impossible!

With their cobra-like hoods extended and rocking back and forth, as if trying to work out how to strike him, which bit of his suit to puncture, the impossible was indeed facing Lukas Minski.

Space snakes.

Lukas wanted to laugh at the ludicrousness of it – but he didn't.

Instead he reached towards his red toolbox.

'Not yet,' he said. 'Please, not yet…'

As one, the snakes lunged across the surface of the Moon towards him, so much faster than anything Lukas had ever seen before. He threw up his hands to protect himself…

CHAPTER 3
LIFE IN A DAY

Three days later, the base Kommandant was reading the report that Bob Moss had submitted before he had returned to Earth (it briefly registered in the Kommandant's mind that no one had actually seen Moss go, but that didn't matter).

Moss had also proven to be as good as the Kommandant had hoped – he'd calmed the two Americans down, got them to stop trying to dominate meetings and also found ways to bring their plans in way under budget. So far under budget that UNIT were considering a couple of other corporations who had submitted ideas that might be even more economically viable. Moss had been responsible for putting their tenders in front of the Kommandant too. What a good man Bob Moss was.

But for now, he was more interested in this report – because it detailed the initial buggy accident, and that Lukas Minski had reported at 1425 CET to repair it.

The architect's team had returned to base but Moss had stayed outside with Minski a few more minutes. His report made mention of the strange phenomena he had seen on the ground, which he had referred to as "snakes".

The Kommandant pressed the delete key, and the references to snakes were obliterated.

It wouldn't be good to have that on anything official at this stage of development. And Moss had signed enough forms to ensure that he'd be locked up for years for breathing a word about this back home.

The Kommandant saved the document and emailed it to HQ, naming it:

FILE LM/dec/Unexp.doc

He attached the one photo, showing the crashed buggy, and Lukas Minski's abandoned spanner just sitting there beside it with a small torn picture.

There was another photo taken shortly afterwards, where the spanner was gone, but its shape was still indented into the dust. As it always would be. The spanner was now in lock-up, evidence along with that photo.

The Kommandant briefly glanced at the photo within the photo, which seemed to show a woman and a young girl by a church. He checked his records – yes, Minski had a wife and daughter. With a heavy heart, the Kommandant knew someone would have to tell them that their husband/father had vanished in an inexplicable manner and should be presumed dead.

They'd get his full benefits of course, but he knew that was really no consolation for Lukas' death.

Maybe he'd ask Bob Moss to go to their house and tell them. He was the last person to speak to Lukas. He could tell them his mood, tell them what he'd told the Kommandant about the birthday and pass on the gift they'd found in Lukas Minski's room.

Yes, he could do it – the English were good at things like that. The Kommandant could always pull the old, "Oh you know us Europeans, we're never the best at breaking the sad news, people say we don't have the empathy," and other nonsense.

He noted that Minski's toolbox was missing from the evidence. A red metal one according to witnesses. The photo and spanner were left behind but Minski, or whoever was responsible for his disappearance, took the toolbox too.

Why?

The Kommandant shut down his computer and sighed.

Snakes indeed.

Space snakes.

On the surface of the Moon.

How ridiculous was that?

He was interrupted by a knock on the door.

'Come.'

It opened and Sergeant Tanner saluted him.

'You look... concerned, Tanner,' the Kommandant said.

'We have an intruder, sir,' Tanner reported. 'At least, I think he is. He says he's here at your request.'

'Who is it?' The Kommandant shut down his tablet and slid it into a drawer.

A small, balding man in a dark suit and carrying an attaché case pushed past Tanner and stood facing the Kommandant.

'I must make a formal complaint, Kommandant,' he said angrily. 'Since I got here, your troops have treated me like a criminal, accusing me of spying, of being an imposter and most of all, refusing to believe my credentials. You asked me here, Kommandant, *you* sort it out.'

The Kommandant looked at Tanner with a shrug, then smiled at the angry newcomer. He was English – always so angry, the English.

'I'm very sorry, but I have no idea what you are talking about,' he said calmly. 'Who are you?'

The Englishman snatched a piece of paper that Tanner was carrying – presumably Tanner had taken it from him earlier.

'There,' he said. 'Look.'

It was an official UNIT docket, giving permission for him to come to the Moon and carry out tasks as required. It bore the Kommandant's signature.

He glanced at the name at the top. 'Is this a joke, Tanner?'

Tanner shook his head. 'Sorry sir, no idea.'

The Kommandant looked at the angry man in front of him. 'And this is you, is it? You are Robert Moss, from the Ministry?'

The man produced a photo ID.

'Yeah, I'm Bob Moss,' he said. 'And you invited me here!'

The Kommandant looked from Moss to Tanner. 'Then who the hell, Sergeant Tanner, was the "Bob Moss" who has been in Moonbase One for the last few days?'

But Sergeant Tanner couldn't answer that.

CHAPTER 4
GREAT LEAP FORWARD

Eight years later – 8 April 2025

Sam took a deep breath and closed his eyes. Why was he first? That was weird. Surely one of the others, one of the grown-ups, should have pushed their way to the front, been all cocky and confident. But they hadn't. They'd sort of let him take the lead this once. Great – thanks everyone.

And that voice he knew came from the very back – but because it was coming through a helmet speaker, it sounded like it was right next to him. Someone was telling him everything was fine and safe – provided he followed "procedures".

Sam found that really, really annoying. For a start: what procedures? Like Sam, or any of them, had actually been listening when the computer read them out. That same voice was now suggesting, oh so politely, that he get a move on.

'Honestly, Sam, we really don't have all day. Literally. We have about six minutes,' said Joe Rivas.

The next voice Sam heard in his helmet was Caitlin's.

'You okay, Sam?'

Of course he wasn't "okay". He was about to climb down from a space shuttle and stand on the Moon. The Moon. Big thing. In the sky. Up there! Well not so "up there" at the moment, more sort of "three metres down below and looking very grey, dusty and a bit scary. A lot scary".

'I'm fine,' Sam somehow spoke back. 'It's just a bit...'

'Yes, I perceive it is,' said another voice. That was Michael. Only he would say "perceive" rather than "know". That was Michael. He was the brainy one who used long words whenever possible.

Sam tentatively put a foot on the ladder of the shuttle and felt it hard beneath him. With a deep breath he turned round so he faced the others and began lowering himself down, from the relative safety of the shuttle towards the surface of the Moon.

He felt rather than saw other feet on the ladder above him as he went down, their footsteps seeming to be heavier and more urgent than his. Obviously not as scared as him, then.

After what seemed like ages, but was probably less than thirty seconds, Sam realised he was at the bottom of the ladder and remembered what they'd said earlier. "Just let go" – the gravity on the Moon meant they could safely drop down to the ground.

Easier said than done.

'Any chance you might let go?' said a voice in his helmet. That was Savannah. Sam always blushed when Savannah spoke directly to him. Thank goodness she couldn't see that while he wore the helmet. He obligingly let go and dropped a tiny distance onto the surface of the Moon.

The *Moon!*

Earth's moon.

Big thing in the sky.

And he was standing on it.

Wow.

Savannah was suddenly standing beside him and then one after another his other two friends, Michael and Caitlin, joined them.

They stared at the ground, at the sky, the shuttle and then across to Moonbase Laika.

'We're here,' Caitlin said in all their ears. 'We are actually here, wow.'

Sam glanced back at the shuttle as the adults started down the ladder.

Hsui Lan was first – the only person to have her national flag, the red square with five gold stars in the top left corner, representing the Peoples' Republic of China, emblazoned on her spacesuit, along with the logo from *Catch A Star*, the international talent show she'd won last Easter. That was everywhere – on her T-shirts, her trainers, the shoulder bag in which she kept her tablet and of course her tablet's wallpaper.

Behind her was Aaron Relevy, the Web Tube sensation, who at the age of ten had so impressed multiplatform companies with his self-broadcast shows from his bedroom that they'd hired him on the spot as a presenter and interviewer for "youth" programming. Now nineteen, he was already considered a veteran of broadcasting the world over – and was compere of *Catch A Star*. His coming on the trip to the Moon was as exciting as it was obvious to Sam. It wasn't possible to imagine anything connected with *Catch A Star* not featuring Aaron. Attached to the side of his head at all times was a home-made webcam, broadcasting everything he saw and heard back to the production base in London, where it would be cut into a series of reality shows for rapid transmission. Aaron was famous the Web over for his inserts where he'd show people how to build things out of discarded rubbish. He built an Mp3 player, a mini-computer drive and a robot dog from bits he found in a rubbish skip at the back of an electronics shop. That one segment of his show had brought him fame, fortune and the chance to host anything he wanted. *Catch A Star* had been his first choice.

However, it had been another of Aaron Relevy's shows that had brought Sam and his other friends to the Moon.

Four months ago the news had made the announcement that World State was launching its first Lunar Transport Shuttle, affordable to all, for regular trips to the Moon.

To mark this occasion, the webcast *BPXtra* had run a competition for kids to design a mural for the Chill-Out Area (whatever that was) on Moonbase Laika. Split into two age categories, the two winners of each bracket would not only see their murals painted in the base, but they'd be the first people to make the public trip in the shuttle, *Yerosha*.

Sam and Savannah were the winners in the 13–16 year old group, Caitlin and Michael were the winners of the 9–12 group.

Aaron Relevy had made the announcement on *BPXtra* one afternoon, and Sam had watched in shock with his mum and dad as the results were revealed.

'You're going to the Moon,' his dad had said quietly. His mum might have just squealed in excitement but had not really said anything that Sam could remember clearly.

The whole street seemed to know within minutes and before long, he was on the local news, and the main page of the *Lichfield Times* website.

The producers of *BPXtra* had arrived the next day, with forms for his parents to fill in, a list of dates Sam would need to be at the old UNEXA training centre in Wolverton to get ready for the flight and a load of requests for appearances on *BPXtra,* plus photo shoots with the other winners for various websites.

As Sam stood on the surface of the Moon, staring across the vast distance to Moonbase Laika, he remembered one other thing that had happened.

He hadn't told anyone about this, including his

parents because at the time it had seemed so silly and, well, mad really.

Sam had been in the *BPXtra* studio canteen with Caitlin and Savannah, getting to know each other and chatting about the training they were doing to be ready for the spaceflight.

Sam had gone to a drinks machine, to get a can of cola, when an old man had walked over.

He looked harmless enough and at first, Sam had thought he was a cleaner or something like that and smiled at him. The man had stopped and lent on the drinks machine, glancing around, like he was worried someone might see him. He stared at Savannah and Caitlin, who were chatting together about some app on Savannah's smartfone, and then came down to Sam's level, eye to eye.

His face was lined, and his cheeks red and blotchy. His hair was streaked grey and white, scraggly and looked like it hadn't been washed in weeks.

He took Sam by the shoulders. 'Listen to me. I don't have much time – they are watching and waiting. You be careful up there, young man,' he said, with a heavy European accent – Polish or Romanian maybe. Sam remembered that his breath had been warm and stale, and Sam had flinched slightly. 'Keep a look out for the red box. And the space snakes. Because they'll be back for it.'

And the man stood up, shook Sam's hand firmly and walked away, towards a door to somewhere that Sam hadn't been. 'Tell no one you saw me or they'll be after you too.' And then he closed his eyes. 'One day, this will all be sorted and, finally, it'll be time to go home,' he said, walking through the door.

Sam never saw him again, and a few seconds later another door had opened and Sam had met Aaron Relevy and Hsui Lan for the first time as they were escorted into the room by some *BPXtra* staff.

He'd put it out of his mind until now. Because as Sam stared at the dusty surface of the Moon for the first time in his life, he was sure that he saw something move out of the corner of his eye.

Maybe it was dust moved by their arrival, a delayed reaction as the ripples of their movement slowly spiralled the dust away. But to Sam it made him think of the bizarre sideways movement snakes made when they moved quickly to avoid human contact.

Perhaps the old man had been right. Perhaps the space snakes were back.

Whatever a space snake was.

CHAPTER 5
CYNICAL HEART

Sym Sergei was a bit of a technical genius. Back home in the Ukraine, his grandmother had always said so. She loved her grandson and was not afraid of coming forward and telling everyone this. People in the street, in the shops, the local bloggers, anyone who would listen.

'Born on these streets,' she'd say. 'And now look at him. Trained in Moscow and America. By the Americans. He's been to MIT even.'

Not that Sym was the first Ukrainian to have done so, but for a grandmother brought up back in the late twentieth century, he had some sympathy with her excitement.

Sym was rather proud of himself, too – but he never liked to display it outwardly. But he had been top of his class at MIT and had published enough papers to make him highly sought after. Going to the Moon had been a long-held ambition, having grown up with his grandparents telling him about all those Russian cosmonauts who had been the first men in space. And when Moonbase Laika (itself named after a Russian dog that had ventured into space more than seventy years ago) had been established by World State, it seemed that his destiny lay up here.

When he'd got the news that World State had accepted him, he went home, hugged his family, collected his uniform from the World State supply department and within a week was settling into his small quarters on the Base. He shared them with a Nigerian systems analyst called Hugo and the two of them had hit it off straight away.

Sym was also an analyst, but whereas Hugo's speciality was spreadsheets and records and stuff, Sym's field was artificial intelligences and programming.

As a result he had been put on the Chief of Science's team, and was one of three people on Moonbase Laika with access to HEART twenty-four/seven.

That was a huge responsibility, as the Chief was forever telling him.

HEART itself was a room at the centre of the base, connected to the outer ring by three long corridors. Between HEART, those corridors and the main base was just empty space.

He remembered his first view of the Base when his shuttle had landed on the Moon. It just looked like a big dome with an outer ring at the base. But once inside, he learned that under the dome, everything wasn't quite so uniform.

For a start there were three major areas, Command Area, the Planetarium (with associated laboratories) and the Mess – three large rooms equidistant from one another – the ringed corridor entering each room and exiting on the other side.

Along those corridors were storerooms,

sleeping quarters, small hydroponic labs to create oxygen, and the filtration systems for food and water recycling.

And then at the centre of everything was HEART, and that was where Sym enjoyed spending as much time as possible.

HEART had three functions. Firstly, it was the literal nerve centre of Moonbase Laika – everything was controlled from within it. Life support, communications, all essential systems were adjusted and maintained by HEART. Secondly, it was a research device, constantly being updated with data that the labs sent it, formulating and distributing information and conclusions, satisfying World States' requirements that Moonbase Laika be a fully operational research station. And thirdly, it was a records store – everything that had occurred in the Base since it was first built right up to date was stored here, accessed via a series of encrypted codes that only the Commander and immediate executive staff could access. Sym himself didn't have that clearance, but nevertheless he was pleased to be one of the HEART operational team. It was a big responsibility but one he embraced.

HEART was a tall, cylindrical room, not especially wide but it went straight up, higher than anywhere else on the Moonbase. Small ladders placed at irregular places enabled an operator to reach a different level of controls. Right at the top, sixty metres up, was the small alcove which only the Chief of Science had clearance codes to go into – that was where the nuclear power core was accessed. Sym's job never required him to go much above thirty metres but a few times he'd climbed all the way up, just for the kick of looking back down. It was a long drop, illuminated by the ever-shifting pattern of lights and glows that HEART gave off. It was almost like the room was breathing in some strange way, as the pulsating lights took on a rhythm if you stared at them long enough, and the best way to observe that was from above.

Right now, Sym was entering a new series of variables for HEART to consider. Recently a number of crewmen had suffered from amnesia.

They'd either woken up in their beds unable to remember how they got there, or would just wander into the Mess or Command Area, dazed after vanishing a few hours earlier.

No one had been able to explain how or why this was happening, but it was concerning to Godfried, the Chief of Security.

Sym was seeing if HEART could detect a pattern to the disappearances, or the people involved and uncover something that human eyes had missed.

He was just entering the exact times and dates of these occurrences when he heard the first sound, a sort of scratching that came from somewhere behind him. He ignored it, probably just some new noise made by HEART's programmes as they chittered and buzzed away. Most people forgot it even made these noises after working there for a while, it just became background white noise.

Then there it was again. The fact that he kept hearing it made him realise it couldn't be HEART or his mind would have filtered it out.

There! Again!

It wasn't inside HEART, but in Corridor 3, the one that was closest to the laboratory areas back in the Ring.

Putting down his tablet, Sym stuck his head back out of HEART and into the corridor. It took a few seconds for his eyes to adjust from the multicoloured haze of HEART to the stark greyness of the corridor.

He looked around. Nothing.

No wait, there it was again... Sym was going to call out but then reckoned if anyone could even hear him back in the Ring, they'd think he was mad.

He looked around and heard the noise again. There. Down by the vent covering.

He dropped to the floor and put his face close to the vent, trying to peer into the darkness. He knew the vent system, it carried recycled air throughout the base in a series of small thin tubes that laced under the surface of the base. The tech crews hated them if they went wrong, they were barely wide enough for a man to get his arm into, so all repairs and maintenance had to be done with remote control devices small enough to travel through the networks.

But that noise was definitely from in there. Was it a remote? One that had been left down there? Unlikely, the tech guys were usually pretty good at tidying up after themselves. But...

Hisssssss.

What was that?

Hisssss.

Sym didn't like that at all. Was that air leaking? He put his hand on the vent grille but felt no pressure, so it wasn't a leak – thank God. If it had been and it wasn't dealt within minutes, the whole Moonbase could be compromised. They might all die from asphyxiation as the air was sucked out of the base and into the vacuum of the surface.

But if it wasn't a pressure leak, what could it be?

He reached into a pocket, took out a small screwdriver and released the grille.

A strange smell wafted into his nostrils and he coughed slightly.

That was weird.

With the grille gone, he could get fractionally closer and look downwards slightly.

A flash of... a flash of silver? Something was moving down there? But that really was mad! Perhaps it was one of the remote-controlled devices that had been left there, picking up a stray signal and trying to move.

He reached into the tiny space with his hand, tapping into the darkness, seeing if he could feel what it was.

And that was when he felt a stab of pain in his hand, and he whipped it back.

At first he assumed he'd caught the side of his hand on something jagged, but goodness knew what. As he looked at his hand, there wasn't a scratch on it. Just two tiny marks, like pinpricks, about two centimetres apart.

And slowly, as he stared at the marks, blobs of his blood oozed from them.

He wiped the blood away and went to stand up, to call a tech crew to deal with this. But he couldn't get up. His legs simply wouldn't push up and he realised he was lying on the floor, panicking.

And then darkness rushed into his mind. Sym's eyes closed and he blacked out.

CHAPTER 6
I TRAVEL

Sam turned and watched the last people to jump out of the craft. They were an odd pair in their mid-twenties. They worked for World State and, when not in space suits, wore pristine pale blue suits, shirts and shoes. Like a couple of cartoon characters, they had fixed smiles that Sam reckoned didn't reach their eyes. It was as if they had been told to be as nice as pie to the kids but really they would rather have been doing anything else. Anywhere else. With anyone else.

Sam could never shake the feeling that underneath their chirpy smiles and, "hey wow kids, we're just as excited as you are, yeah?" attitude, twins Joe and Jo Rivas were hating every minute of this experience.

And that made Sam smile, because he didn't like either of them. They were, they explained, there to "protect the brand" which after Caitlin asked for an explanation, they learned meant that World State considered the Lunar Transport Shuttle to be something big and important. 'It's like when you see a Batman movie or a James Bond film,' Jo had smiled insincerely. 'A big on-going thing like that, with logos and names that people recognise the world over, that's a brand. And it's our job to make sure that everyone enjoys the brand and what happens doesn't spoil it, or disrespect it in any way.'

'That makes it crystal clear,' Savannah had sneered. 'Thanks for that.'

Michael had put his hand up, and successfully caught Jo and Joe's attention. 'Yes?'

'Strictly speaking, Batman and James Bond aren't "brands" they are franchises,' he said. 'On-going movie series like that are —'

And Joe had cut across him. 'Yes, well, it's all very complicated I'm sure, but basically it means we have to make sure that nothing on this trip to the Moon reflects badly on either World State or, more importantly, our new, exciting and thrilling Lunar Transport Shuttle program.'

Michael shrugged and shut up.

Now, they were all stood together at the airlock.

Sam recalled the schematics he'd seen on Moonbase Laika. It was basically like a huge bicycle wheel – the main area being the "wheel", a long circular corridor. Along the way the wheel had "bumps" – these were a series of important rooms, which he remembered included things like laboratories, canteens, and bigger places such as the "Chill-out" Area and the famous Command Area, which Michael had kept telling Sam he really wanted to see. Also on the corridor, on either side, were a series of cabins for the crew to sleep in.

Then, leading from the wheel, were three long "spokes" that led to a central hub that stretched right up, but Sam didn't know what that was – it wasn't labelled on the schematics.

Excited by what was about to happen, what they were all about to see, Sam smiled as Joe reached forward and pressed a large green square on the wall. Perhaps it was the doorbell, he thought.

Sure enough, a moment later, the outer door to the airlock opened with a big hiss they could hear through their suits before the vacuum of space deadened the sound completely. They all filed in and the door closed again.

'Four minutes,' Jo said in their helmets. Sam knew that was how long it would take for the cubicle they were in to be filled with oxygen, after which they would be able to take off their suits.

It was a very slow four minutes in which no one said very much. Aaron made a joke about the decor (it was grey, a lot of grey) and Caitlin asked if the World State was planning trips to Mars, to which Jo laughed quickly and said Caitlin was a very clever little girl for asking such a very clever question. No actual answer though.

Sam could hear the hiss as the air seeped into the

cubicle and focussed on that, knowing that once it stopped hissing, that meant it was just a further minute from being time to get out of their suits.

It was actually a minute and a half before Jo and Joe said they could remove their helmets, presumably just making sure. After all, Sam guessed, it wouldn't do their "brand" much good if they killed four kids and two web celebrities before they'd even got through the door of the Moonbase by suffocating them.

The inner door of the airlock opened when Joe Rivas turned a huge plastic wheel in the centre of the door. It reminded Sam of the ones he'd seen on submarines in movies.

And then Sam and the others got their first view of the interior of Moonbase Laika.

It was exactly the opposite of what Sam had expected. He had imagined futuristic white corridors, carpets, hexagonal designs on the walls, maybe plants in red plastic vases.

But it looked nothing like the movies he'd watched in preparation. This was the long curved corridor – the "wheel" he'd seen on the schematics, but it was so... *sterile*.

Basically Moonbase Laika was mostly bland steel and plastic girders holding pale blue squares in place that acted like big building blocks. A Lego Moonbase, he thought, where everything was curved so you could only see the next few metres ahead if you kept moving. Jo and Joe Rivas almost seemed to melt into the walls, the blue of their suits and the walls being identical. Branding, he guessed.

They marched off down a corridor, a lit up sign saying MESS and a red arrow pointing in the direction they were going.

Sam turned to Savannah. 'Exciting, yeah?'

She nodded, her eyes glittering as she took it all in.

Behind them, he could hear Aaron and Hsui passing comment about the place, whilst just ahead, Michael was walking between Jo and Joe. He was pointing things out as they passed them, displaying an amazing amount of knowledge about how this was constructed, or why that was shaped the way it was, or how the original plans for the Base had changed because of this, that and the other. Sam liked Michael because, although he rarely shut up, he did know about stuff. Then there was the fact that it also probably annoyed the Rivas twins, as he clearly knew more than they did.

After a while they found themselves outside the Mess, which Sam now realised meant "canteen".

'Okay people,' Joe Rivas started, then stopped. 'Umm, where are Aaron and Hsui?'

Sam realised that he hadn't noticed the web stars weren't with them once they began walking down the curving corridor. Joe threw his sister a look that might have been saying "Whose job was it to keep an eye on these people?".

She smiled at them. 'I expect they've seen something interesting that we missed. I'll go find them, while Joe takes you in for a... fizzy drink.'

'They probably won't have carbonated drinks on Moonbase Laika,' Michael explained to her. 'The atmospheric displacement means that –'

'Whatever,' Jo smiled slightly tighter. 'You lot go in and settle down, I'll find the other two.'

Sam and Michael however chose to follow her – canteens were so boring, and Sam wasn't hungry. He wanted to see more of this place, and knew Michael was thinking the same way. They followed Jo as she walked back down the corridor, retracing the way they'd come but they didn't get very far before voices floated towards them.

'So, what, you just started strumming a guitar and making up songs about comic books?' said a man's voice Sam hadn't heard before.

'That's right.' That was Aaron. 'Put it up on the web and got four million hits in the first week.'

'Wow,' said the newcomer, as Aaron, Hsui and he came around the curved corridor. 'I'm impressed. And I'm not easily impressed. Unless you can do that magic trick where you put a phone inside a beer bottle now *that* is impressive – and I've never worked out how to do it.'

The newcomer was tall, dark-haired and quite young although he wore an old-fashioned jacket and bow tie. He waved his arms around when he talked, wriggling his fingers all the time, too.

He glanced towards Sam, and presumably the others, but to Sam it seemed that he was looking straight at him with the most amazing blue eyes that glistened and almost shone with... something that made Sam grin.

'And you? Hsui was it? Loved your album, the one with the picture of the swans on it.'

Hsui looked at him and shrugged. 'But... it's not out yet. We haven't even revealed the cover to anyone.'

The newcomer made an exaggerated "oh" look with his face. 'Sorry,' he said. 'My mistake.'

'No, but the cover *will* have swans on it,' she said. 'How did you know?'

The newcomer shrugged. 'Oh, lucky guess I expect. You look like a swans kind of girl, and... people... like swans I think. Hope. Imagine. Probably.'

'Who are you?' Jo Rivas finally asked.

The newcomer produced a small wallet with

some kind of ID in it. He was too far away for Sam to see what it said, but he heard the reply. 'Ministry of Moons and Moonbases. Very new. Very... exclusive. Been sent up here to check up on things, make sure everything is hunky dory and that the, ummm, yes, the children here have a safe and educational tour.' He smiled at them all again, then leaned towards Jo. 'I assume education plays a part in all this, it's not all ice cream and fizzy pop?'

With an exaggerated sigh, Michael started again. 'They can't have carbonated drinks because –'

'Yes, yes,' said the strange man. 'Atmospherics and all that. Complete nonsense of course. Provided the gravity is set correctly, nothing to stop you having lemonade, cola and ginger beer till your heart's content actually.' He was close enough to nudge Michael's shoulder now, which he did playfully. 'But ten out of ten for knowing about such things. You are going to be very useful to me, I reckon.' He looked at the rest of them. 'You all are, I'm sure.' He then lent forward and pointed back at the Rivas twins with his thumb. 'Except

I'm not sure about the blue suits here, they look a bit grumpy to me.'

Joe Rivas stepped forward. 'Excuse me...?'

'Doctor,' he said. 'I'm the Doctor. From the Ministry of –'

'I heard,' said Joe. 'Now look, I – what *are* you doing?'

The Doctor had dropped to the floor and Sam was surprised to see him tapping at a small air vent between the wall and floor. He even seemed to sniff it. Then it was as if he remembered the others were there and he stopped sniffing, looked up at everyone and grinned rather sheepishly. 'What were you saying?'

'That I didn't know you were going to be here,' said Joe.

'Oh. Well, sorry. But that's not really my fault. Should have been on your itinerary.'

'What itinerary?' asked Jo.

'Well, there you are then,' smiled the Doctor, as if that solved everything. 'I was on the itinerary you don't have. See how easily things fall apart without itineraries and plans and stuff?'

Sam found himself grinning at the way this Doctor managed to poke fun at the Rivas twins without actually being rude to them.

'So come on then, let's get this party started,' the Doctor said. 'Lead on.'

Jo Rivas raised her eyes towards the ceiling, took a deep breath and then shrugged. 'This way,' she sighed and they quickly joined the rest of the group in the cafeteria.

Sam looked the Doctor up and down as they re-entered, and he in turn looked down at Sam, and winked. 'Hullo. Excited to be in outer space?'

Sam nodded. 'It's brill

The Doctor grinned. 'You know what, it is, isn't it? The most brilliant thing ever.'

'What were you doing, sniffing at that vent?'

'Oh,' said the Doctor. 'Oh, you noticed me doing that.'

Sam shrugged. 'Kind of think we all did.'

The Doctor pointed down at another vent. 'Air vents. For recycled air. Useful on a Moonbase.'

Sam agreed, adding, 'But why the sniffing?'

The Doctor stared at Sam, as if making his mind up whether or not to tell him something. Something Sam felt might be very important. 'I'm testing a theory that's been bugging me ever since I arrived here a couple of hours ago. Something on the tip of my...'

'Tongue?'

'No,' replied the Doctor. 'Tip of my mind. She can be so frustrating sometimes, never tells me anything.'

'She?' asked Sam.

'The TARDIS. My ship. She gets a bit moody sometimes and presumably brought me back here for a reason. No real idea what though. Have you?'

'Nope,' Sam said.

The Doctor wandered to a porthole in the wall, but before following him, Sam dropped down to the vent and gave it a sniff. Nothing weird there, so perhaps – wait!

But... but that was impossible...

'Intriguing, isn't it?' asked the Doctor, without

actually looking at Sam.

Sam immediately scurried over to him, joining the Doctor looking outside onto the expanse of greyness that was the Moon's surface.

'What did the vent tell you?' he asked Sam, still not looking at him.

'I... but... nah, it's stupid.'

The Doctor looked at Sam finally, with something like disappointment on his face. 'Oh,' he said. 'Oh, okay.'

Sam didn't want to disappoint this strange man. 'I heard... I heard sounds.'

'What sort of sounds?' the Doctor asked.

Sam shrugged. 'Just noises. Like something moving. Breathing perhaps? But that's impossible. Nothing can be in an air vent, can it?'

'On Moonbase Laika?' asked the Doctor. 'No, no course not. Unless...'

'Unless what?'

'Unless there is, unless there is.'

Sam glanced back at the vent, slightly alarmed by the Doctor's words.

Changing the subject, the Doctor drew Sam's attention to the surface of the Moon again. 'What do you see out there?' he asked.

Sam shrugged. 'Dust. The shuttle. Umm, more dust. And Earth in space.'

'Amazing,' the Doctor said. 'Look over there, that large crater, slightly deeper than the others. That's Armstrong, named after the first human to set foot here, on this satellite.'

Sam smiled. 'I bet it's great to have craters named after you.'

The Doctor nodded. 'It's great the first few hundred times. And the second few hundred. And the... well, anyway, yes it never gets boring.'

'It must have been great to be Neil Armstrong. "One small step for man..." and all that.' Sam recalled seeing the footage on the web, all grey and grainy but so awesome.

'Nice man, very smart and no ego,' the Doctor said. 'We had blueberry muffins once. He will always live on in history. So will Buzz Aldrin, immortalised in all those photos that Armstrong took. And Michael Collins, the first man to get furthest away from Earth, the first to see the dark side of the Moon. Fantastic achievements all three. And all the others that followed, but those three were the lunar pioneers that made this place possible.' The Doctor sighed slightly, then pointed again out of the window. 'Now, shall I tell you what else I can see?'

Sam stared harder. There was nothing else to see.

'Each grain of dust just sits there,' the Doctor said, 'unmoving, untouched even by solar winds. Just over there, protected by a small plastic dome, is Neil Armstrong's footprint. And off to the left is a crater where the UNIT cosmonauts that built this base started measuring the Moon out. The compass one of them dropped is still there, on its end. And then, oh just look at that dust. You see grey. I see colours, millions of different shades, each grain of dust telling a story about history, about the formation of the solar system, the whole universe. Some of them have been telling that story for millions of years, but no one ever listens.' He paused, then looked back at Sam. 'I'm just talking rubbish,' he said. 'Ignore me.'

But Sam was captivated. If he squinted he was sure he could see silver and blue and green rather than just grey in the dust. And he was thinking about the footprint and the compass. 'It's beautiful,' he breathed. 'It's the Moon!'

The Doctor grinned broadly. 'Oh I like you... whoever you are.'

'Sam. Sam Miller.'

The Doctor shook his hand. 'Good to meet you, Sam Miller. You and I are going to be good mates, I reckon.'

The Doctor wandered over to the others and Sam threw one last look outside onto the magical surface of the Moon.

And then, just for a brief second, he thought he saw something move. Just slightly, as if some of that space dust that the Doctor had reckoned was unmoving after all the centuries, shimmered and shifted.

It was probably just light reflecting, Sam told himself. After all, nothing was alive out there, was it?

And again, Sam was suddenly thinking about the old man's warning about Space Snakes. And the vents, the noise, the breathing, the Doctor sniffing.

He looked outside again, but everything was still and untouched. Just as it had been forever.

Because nothing could live on the surface of the Moon. Especially not snakes.

CHAPTER 7
LET THE CHILDREN SPEAK

Sam and the others were drinking some strange fruit drink in the cafe. It had little taste, despite the fruits painted on the label and the promises of nutrition, energy and vitamin C.

Sam chucked his into a box marked "waste" and nearly jumped out of his skin when it was immediately all but sucked out of his hand by a fierce gust of noisy wind.

'Ah,' said Michael. 'Vacuum disposal chutes. They take the waste and shred it into powder,' he smiled at Sam. 'Don't fall in after it.'

'I won't,' said Sam, gingerly moving away from the chute.

Jo and Joe were tapping on their smartfones and at first Sam thought they were playing a game, but he soon realised they were messaging people. Perhaps someone else on the base. Or maybe World State HQ back on Earth. It occurred to Sam that they might be checking up on the strange Doctor from the Ministry of Moons and Moonbases, when both he and Savannah walked into the cafe.

'Toilets are that way,' Savannah said, as if to explain their absence.

'Vacuum?' asked Michael.

Savannah nodded slowly in a way that suggested she hadn't been expecting toilets quite so... ferocious.

Aaron and Caitlin were reading some notices on the wall – some were electronic, others written by hand and attached with some kind of sticky plastic material.

'Apparently some of our murals are going in here,' Caitlin said, frowning.

'Well, that's nice,' said Hsui. 'Brighten this place up no end.'

'I wanted them to go in the Chill-Out Area,' said Caitlin. 'That's what *BPXtra* promised.'

'No they didn't,' responded Jo Rivas, carefully putting her own drinks carton in the waste, having seen Sam's surprise earlier. 'They just hoped they might be.'

'Still,' said the Doctor cheerily, looking at each kid in turn. 'Still, could be worse. Could be the toilets they put them in.'

Jo and Joe Rivas threw him a look as if to say "great, that helps," then went back to their phones.

'Well,' the Doctor continued, 'shouldn't someone from the base have met us by now?'

'Just what we're checking on,' muttered Joe.

Aaron sidled over to Hsui.

'You okay?' he asked.

The Chinese girl nodded and Sam noticed she seemed to turn away slightly, staring briefly at the tabletop, the ground and then finding a salt-shaker quite interesting. Anything but catching Aaron's eye.

Sam smiled to himself. It had become obvious to everyone recently that Aaron fancied Hsui and

Hsui fancied him back – but they were both too shy to actually say anything to each other.

But the presenter was getting braver now it seemed. 'Fancy a quick wander?'

'Sounds like fun. I'll come with you,' said Sam.

'No,' said Aaron.

'Yes,' said Hsui at the same time.

'Ok,' said Aaron, shooting Sam a look that immediately made Sam wish he'd not said a word – and Sam realised that they probably wanted to be alone. But it was too late to take it back now.

'Actually, no, you can't,' said Joe. 'Everyone stay here, we can't go wandering around Moonbase Laika like we own the place.'

'I thought you did,' said Caitlin. 'World State, anyway. And you are from World State...'

'We work for World State,' Jo said. 'Not the same as owning this place.'

'Too right,' said a new voice. They all turned to look at the doorway. There was a man standing there, in a one-piece red overall. A number of insignia sewn into the chest area made him look very grand.

Which was a contrast to the man himself, who looked not much older than Aaron. Both Joe Rivas and the Doctor were probably older than him.

He had short blond hair, blue eyes and a cheerful smile that made his eyes sparkle, as if they were permanently watery.

'Hi there everyone,' he replied. 'I'm Godfried.' He had a very slight accent that Sam tried to place. European definitely. German, or maybe Dutch?

The Rivas twins were walking towards him, hands outstretched ready to shake, with an eagerness Sam hadn't seen in them before.

'Mr Christoffel,' Jo Rivas said. 'A pleasure. I'm Jo. This is Joe.'

The newcomer nodded. 'Ah yes, we spoke over webchat,' he said. 'Thank you for bringing the children to Moonbase Laika. I hope the trip was easy.'

'World State craft are always comfortable,' Joe Rivas said, like it was something he'd learned to say in these situations. 'It's what makes World State so popular with travellers.'

Godfried Christoffel paused before answering. 'Of course,' he finally said.

'And now, we are anxious to head back to Earth as soon as possible.'

The surprise from the other visitors and even the Doctor was expressed vocally, loudly and all at once.

'Okay, okay, okay,' Joe finally quietened everyone down. 'We were never going to stay up here with you. World State got you here and we'll send another shuttle in three days to collect you. Our job is done.' He smiled as if that was the best news he'd ever heard. 'After all, you are perfectly safe here, in a World State Moonbase, with Mr Christoffel's crew. He's Chief of Security, you see.'

'Why do you need security on a Moonbase?' asked Michael.

Jo Rivas smiled at Christoffel. 'This is Michael. He asks a lot of questions.'

'Good ones,' the Doctor observed.

'And that's the Doctor. But presumably you've met.'

Christoffel looked at the Doctor. 'No.'

'Of course we haven't,' the Doctor stood up and walked over to him, flashing his strange little pass at him. 'Ministry of Moons and Moonbases. The Doctor. Hullo.' And he winked at Christoffel. 'And now we have. Met, that is. Marvellous.'

He wandered back to where he had been sitting and put his feet up on a chair. 'Great Moonbase by the way. I'll be giving the canteen ten out of ten in my report, no problems.'

'Ministry of what?' asked the Chief of Security. 'I have never heard of it.'

'Course you haven't,' the Doctor said. 'Be a bit silly if you had – we could hardly do surprise inspections of all the Moonbases if you knew we existed. And were visiting.'

'We are the *only* Moonbase. Anywhere. Why is there a Ministry of them?'

'Brand new,' the Doctor carried on. 'Only launched last month. Do you like that? Launched – like a space rocket. Deliberate choice of words, you see, all to do with the PR. I'm sure the Rivas family here can tell you all how important good PR is. And branding. And franchising. And... anyway, I'm sure your Commander will be expecting me. Probably told to keep it all hush-hush from everyone. Just ignore me, pretend I'm not here and everything will be fine.'

Godfried Christoffel breathed out heavily and turned back to the Rivas twins. 'Anyway, I'm sorry but no, you can't go.'

'What?'

'Of course we can!' Jo Rivas looked at her brother, as if he would magically change Christoffel's mind.

'It's the sunspots,' Christoffel explained. 'The course away from the Moon back home would need to be a different trajectory to avoid them, but because of the debris orbiting Earth and where the pockets of safe passage are through them, they're not aligned right now. You'll be here at least three days, so I've cancelled the other shuttle and you can all go home together after all.'

Sam took some pleasure in the obvious

discomfort Jo Rivas felt at this news, although he wasn't sure why. Maybe it was because she had been so keen to dump them on the Moon and leave them here without actually telling anyone that had been the plan.

Her brother, however, was more upset than that. 'You don't understand, Chief, we have to get away from here today.'

Christoffel shrugged. 'Sorry. Not going to happen.'

'Oh dear,' said the Doctor with a wink to Sam and the others. 'Looks like we're all in this together. Shame World State didn't do something about all that space junk orbiting Earth beforehand, eh?'

'Space junk?' asked Caitlin.

The Doctor beamed at her. 'Over the last sixty odd years, since mankind started sending satellites and spaceships and skylabs into space, the rockets that get them there get abandoned, left to float in Earth's atmosphere. After so many missions, Earth is ringed by loads and loads of old debris that hasn't burned up in the atmosphere yet. It's hazardous and wasteful. Funny thing is, your planet is all very good and conscientious when it comes to recycling paper and stuff, but utterly pants at it up here in outer space. Wait another hundred years and you'll see you have the most awful reputation with the Galactic Federation as mucky puppies who don't clean up after yourselves.'

'"Galactic Federation"?' asked Hsui.

Sam was more taken by the Doctor's "your planet" comment, but before he could raise it, the Doctor was on his feet, arms around Aaron Relevy's shoulder, steering him out into the corridor and towards the portholes. The others slowly followed.

'See that, Aaron?'

'Yup. That's Earth.'

'Beautiful, isn't it?'

'Stunning,' said Hsui, and Sam noticed she was finally standing as close to Aaron as possible. 'Isn't it stunning?'

'Oh yes,' said the Doctor. But it's ringed by all this awful rubbish that you can't see from here. It's dangerous and will end up needing to be cleared, or you'll find yourselves unable to go back and forth to the Moon, Mars or wherever you want to go without crashing into old *Soyuz*, *Apollo* or *Guinevere* bric-a-brac. Now, you could do yourself a lot of good by setting up a nice special programme watched by billions of kids all over Earth that tells them how important it is to keep space tidy and maybe those that grow up to be scientists and mission controllers and astronauts will stop making such a garbage patch of your atmosphere.'

'Explorers in space,' Hsui said. 'We should be proud of everyone who has ever set foot up here.'

Aaron smiled at her. 'Absolutely.'

The Doctor paused for a second, then grinned at them both, patted them both on the back and somehow as he turned away had managed to link their arms around each others' waists.

'I do so love international romance,' he whispered quietly, so only Sam and Caitlin could hear.

'Anyway,' Joe Rivas said, 'that has nothing to do

with World State and –'

"'Nothing to do with World State"?' echoed the Doctor as he stood in front of Joe, towering over him slightly, and fiddling with his bow tie.

'It has everything to do with World State. You people should be leading the charge, not ignoring it. That, Joseph Rivas, is why the Ministry sent me. To check up on you, and your World State's attitude to such things. And I have to say, I think my Ministry are going to be very disappointed in you.' He threw a look at Jo. 'Both of you.'

Joe swallowed hard and opened his mouth to speak but all that came out was a high-pitched squeak.

Jo Rivas stepped in and smiled at the Doctor. 'Of course, you're right, we apologise.' Then she steered her brother back to a seat in the Mess.

Christoffel gave the Doctor a look that suggested he enjoyed seeing the Rivas's taken down a peg or two. 'Doctor, I'm glad the Ministry sent you up – but I apologise that somewhere along the way communications have got scrambled and we were unaware you would be here. But I am delighted that you are. It'll be a pleasure to have you see how well we have adapted the old base from its original use to what we have today.'

'What was it used for originally?' asked Hsui.

'I know,' said Michael proudly.

Christoffel smiled at him. 'Go ahead, Michael, what do you think it was?'

Michael seemed to grow an inch or two as he answered, pleased to be asked for his knowledge rather than always having to force it on people.

'This base was set up in 2006 by the Unified Intelligence Taskforce as a tracking station, keeping an eye not just on Earth but out into space, a sort of early warning system in case of alien invasion.'

Joe Rivas was back beside them in an instant, eager to spin a bit of PR. 'Almost right. It was more of a scientific research station, exploring new ways to harness solar power, gravitational power and possible mineral sources to replace those we were running out of down on Earth – no one wants to run out of oil before we have a substitute. Then in

2023, UNIT passed it over to World State, because Private Enterprise could fund the research even better. And that is us. And now, thanks to all of you, this base will stop looking quite so militaristic and more... comfortable and friendly. The people who work here were all very excited by your murals.' Joe looked at Christoffel. 'Maybe it's time to meet the staff?'

For some reason everyone turned to look at the Doctor, as if asking his permission or something.

He, however, was stood there, tapping away on a device slightly larger than a Smartphone.

Christoffel put his hand to his pocket and then reached out and took the device away from the Doctor.

'Mine, I think,' he said, half-cross and half-bemused. When exactly had the Doctor managed to take it out of his pocket without him noticing?

'Interesting stuff,' the Doctor smiled.

'What is?' asked Christoffel.

'Oh, you know what I mean.' He gently poked Christoffel in the chest. 'We need some answers, don't we, Chief?'

The Doctor turned on his heel, hands wiggling above his head. 'This way, I believe,' he said and walked on.

Shaking his head, Christoffel suggested they all follow him and prepare to meet the Commander of Moonbase Laika. He started off at a bit of a pace.

Sam and Caitlin found themselves alongside the Doctor as he walked. He was looking around at walls, doors, windows, signs and anything else, muttering quietly and sometimes nodding.

After a few moments, Sam realised the Doctor was addressing the two of them, but quietly. 'You seem like intelligent children. For humans. Oh, you don't mind being called children do you? I'm never sure I get that right – at what point you stop wanting to be called "children", "kids", "offspring", "die kinder", "les enfants" –'

Sam could imagine this going on for a while so he butted in. 'No, children is fine,' he said quietly. 'What did you find out from the Chief's smartphone thingie?'

The Doctor tapped the side of his nose. 'Things.'

'Like about the vents?' asked Sam.

'I like the way you think, Sam. Yes, possibly. People have apparently been disappearing.'

Caitlin gasped.

'Oh, don't worry,' the Doctor carried on. 'They come back, but with gaps in their memories. Just a few hours here and there. Random people, no obvious connection, no links.'

'Other than the fact they work here,' said Sam.

'Well, they'd have to,' said Caitlin. 'There's no one else here except the Moonbase Laika staff.'

'And us,' the Doctor corrected.

'And... and maybe someone else?' offered up Sam.

'Maybe,' the Doctor agreed. 'But let's not worry about it.' Then he threw his arms around their shoulders as they walked. 'So, intelligent little offspring of humans, whose explanation did you prefer? Michael's or Mr Rivas'?'

'Perhaps they were both right?' suggested Caitlin.

'Oh. Oh that's very good. Very observant. Well done.' He smiled at Caitlin, and then turned to Sam. 'Girls, eh. So boring, even when they're right. No sense of adventure.'

'Oi!' said Caitlin. 'Girls are not boring. Girls happen to be brill.'

'Oh. Sorry. Silly me.'

'But,' Sam said, 'she's right. They might both be accurate. But I think Michael's was more... interesting.'

'Oh, it was,' said the Doctor. 'And your World State Brand Team Franchise-Holding PR Gurus over there were a little too quick to give us the approved spiel. Because there's one other thing I want to know about this base that no one has mentioned.'

'What's that?' asked Caitlin.

'Why did UNIT give it up?' the Doctor looked up at the ceiling. 'I mean, they built it, funded it, and used it for a long time. I'm very surprised that they handed it over unless World State offered them a lot of money.'

'World State does have a lot of money,' said Michael, joining them. 'Couldn't help overhearing.'

'So the question remains,' the Doctor carried on, 'why? Why did UNIT sell it and why did World State buy it from them?'

Sam took a deep breath. 'Maybe UNIT didn't like the space snakes.'

The Doctor just shrugged.

'Possibly,' he said. 'Very possibly.'

Caitlin looked horrified and Michael snorted. 'Space snakes? What space snakes?'

'I have no idea at all,' the Doctor grinned. 'But if Sam here thinks it might be because of the space snakes, then we should find out if they really exist.'

'He's just made them up,' Caitlin said.

'Have you just made them up?' the Doctor asked.

Sam shook his head and told them a bit about the old man he'd met in the *BPXtra* studio, and his warning.

'See?' said the Doctor. 'Sounds like space snakes to me.'

'He might have been mad,' said Savannah.

'Or drunk,' added Caitlin.

'Or lying.' That was Michael's contribution.

The Doctor nodded. 'He might also have been giving Sam here a warning for a very good reason. Best not ignore it, just in case. Let's see what the Commander of this base has to say about space snakes when we get there.'

'And if he doesn't believe us?'

The Doctor shrugged. 'Then we'll ask about space cats, space bears, space badgers and even space alpacas. I'll wear him down – I'm good at that.'

'Okay everyone,' Godfried Christoffel called back. 'You are now entering the main control area. Please do not touch anything.'

Sam gave the Doctor a look.

'What?'

Caitlin gave him a similar look.

'You have only known me five minutes!' the Doctor protested. 'Why do you think that applies to *me* any more than you?'

Michael gave him the look.

'Oh, all right,' sulked the Doctor, and shoved his hands into his trouser pockets. 'Happy now?'

Christoffel turned the wheel on the door and swung it outwards, and everyone peered into the Command Area.

It was a circular room, with a couple of doors opposite where they stood now, on the far side.

Seated at a series of individual desks were men and women working on touchscreen surfaces that lit up as they worked, reflecting a variety of colours and images on to their faces. Each of them wore overalls in reds, blues and yellows.

On the right-hand side, the wall was just a massive window, giving a fantastic view of the surface of the Moon. Earth could be seen floating in the pitch blackness of the starless sky. Sam was staring at the vista.

'Wow,' he said. 'Just...wow...'

At which point a tall, dark woman in a green overall stood up from behind a desk with lots of touchscreen controls on it.

'Good afternoon everyone,' she said with a deep American accent that made Sam think of a country and western singer. 'Welcome to Moonbase Laika. My name is Morrison Cann. I'm the Commander and unless you listen very carefully to what I have to say, every single one of you will be dead before nightfall.'

And she smiled at them.

CHAPTER 8
SPACEFACE

Sam looked around him, and nearly everyone looked the same – mouths hanging open, surprise or fear in their eyes.

Oh good, at least it wasn't just him then.

Except Michael. Michael, the brainbox of the gang, he didn't seem worried.

Nor did the Doctor.

So if the Doctor wasn't frightened, there was no need for Sam to be.

He took a deep breath and exhaled. Then he smiled at Savannah. This made her relax a bit too. Sam found he was smiling a bit more.

'Okaaaay,' said Joe Rivas. 'I'm sure Commander

Cann is joking...'

'Absolutely not,' the Commander replied in a firm, matter-of-fact voice. 'And now I have your attention, let me explain what I mean.' She tapped a finger on a wall and a touchscreen glowed into life. On it was a circular diagram that Sam realised was a geometric map of Moonbase Laika.

'Moonbase Laika,' Cann said, 'is a working station. And we expend a great deal of energy up here, keeping the lights, life support, hydroponics etc. all going. It's how we stay alive on a day-to-day basis. But to achieve that, we have to have strict energy saving routines.' She tapped a number of the squares that Sam took to represent rooms on the map. They immediately went red. 'These areas are out of bounds after 9pm CET. So anything marked in red, to preserve what we need, are what we call dead zones. At night when this area is manned by a skeleton staff, we shut down life support in these areas. There's no admittance to them. Don't try, don't think it's a challenge, or a game, it's not. The areas have Hardinger Seals on them, but even so, accidents do happen. If that accident involves you, I won't be writing a sad letter to your parents expressing my sadness at your instantaneous death, I'll be writing to say how stupid you were and deserved it because you didn't listen.'

'Seems harsh,' said Jo Rivas.

'It is harsh, Miss Rivas, because life on the Moon is harsh. It's not like some science fiction movie – in this place the slightest change in routine can kill. The base is set up to support a certain number of staff. Every time we have visitors, we have to adjust the artificial oxygen supply, the gravity, the food rations, everything. We can't just pop down to the nearest 7-11 for supplies, you know.' She looked at them all in turn. Sam felt her eyes burning into him, almost challenging him to defy her. Sam had no intention of doing so. 'You think I'm being harsh? That's nothing to what happens if you die here. I might tell your parents that your death was instantaneous – it's not. It's painful, takes about three minutes to go unconscious and before you do so, your eyes, ears and skin will have ruptured and you will be in agony. And then you die.'

She reached over to a tall red-haired man, in a red overall like Christoffel's, who was tapping some numbers into a touchscreen at a console. 'Lew?'

The man passed her a pile of papers, barely giving Sam's group a glance as he did so before returning to whatever it was he was doing.

The Commander passed the papers to the Rivas twins. 'Distribute these to your party please. It's a print-out of dos and don'ts. A list of what rooms everyone is sleeping in and places of interest to go, places of danger to avoid. Again, I repeat, this is not a challenge. I'm glad you guys are here, and as one of the judges of the competition *BPXtra* ran, I look forward to meeting you all individually and having a laugh. But right now, it's important you understand exactly how dangerous this place is before you find out how great it is too.'

Nervously, Joe Rivas passed the papers around. 'Take one, pass it on,' he said.

Sam read his. Sure enough, it was a copy of the map with each room numbered, and a list of things not to do and places to go. The base seemed very simple, each room clearly marked. The one they were in at the moment was 1, the last room on the list was 37.

There was one place on the wall map that wasn't duplicated on the paper version. Instead it was just marked by a series of criss-cross patterns and no number.

'Excuse me,' he asked nervously.

Commander Cann stared at him, as if sizing him up. 'It's Sam, isn't it?' she finally said.

Sam was taken aback by that, as he assumed was everyone else. How did she know his name?

'I make it my job to read up on everyone World State send up to visit my base,' she said, clearly seeing his confusion.

'Err, right,' he said. 'I just wondered what this room is.' He held the map up.

Cann again called to the red-haired man. He looked across at the group, over the top of his glasses, like a teacher trying to spot a troublemaker.

When he spoke, his voice bore no resemblance

to his size and stature – he had a soft, almost hard to hear Welsh accent.

'Hi there. I'm Llewellyn Hughes, I'm the Chief of Science on Moonbase Laika. And what the young man has asked about is HEART.' He reached out and tapped the wall and a screen appeared. 'This is HEART,' he continued. 'It's the nerve centre of the base, the computer control. Everything that exists here works because of HEART.'

'If it's a computer,' said Michael, 'shouldn't it be called BRAIN?'

Hughes shrugged. 'Brains stop, but the body keeps going. Hearts stop, that's it. Everything withers and dies. Without HEART, this base is dead. That's why no one goes near it. No one except me and my immediate staff. Kindly stay away from it.'

'Well,' said the Doctor, 'that's all very straightforward. Whatever next?'

Commander Cann crossed to the big window. 'I'd like to show our talented group here where their murals are going to end up across the Moonbase.'

All smiles now that she'd delivered her scary pep talk, Cann began ushering everyone towards a door at the rear of the room.

Sam and Savannah hung back a bit, staying close to the Doctor because, somehow, Sam felt like that was a good idea.

He watched as Cann and the others disappeared into the corridor. There would be an opportunity to catch up later. Right now, he wanted to spend more time with the Doctor.

The Doctor and Chief Hughes stared at each other for a moment.

'What if something happens to you, Chief Hughes? Who looks after HEART then?'

The Chief of Science just smiled at him. 'I make sure nothing ever does. But I appreciate your concern, Mr...?'

'Doctor. With a "the".'

Hughes and a couple of other people in the room momentarily stopped what they were doing and looked at the Doctor. Aware that he was being stared at, the Doctor coughed slightly and fiddled with his shirt collar and shuffled the shoulders of his jacket.

'Anyway,' the Doctor continued, 'just, you know, be careful.' He ushered Savannah and Sam forward. 'Come along young adult people-things, let's catch up with the others.'

As they passed Godfried Christoffel, the young Chief of Security tapped the Doctor's arm. 'Where are you from again?'

'Ministry of Moons and Moonbases,' said Sam automatically.

'Yes,' the Doctor agreed, 'Ministry of what my mate Sam said.' The Doctor beamed at Sam. 'See, mates. Told you.'

Sam grinned back.

Christoffel was less impressed. 'Why are you really here, Doctor? Moonbase Laika is a very safe and secure place.'

The Doctor regarded him carefully, then spun around glancing at each and every person in the Command Area, about twelve people in total. Most were just working but Hughes and the others who had caught his glance earlier were all intently watching the Doctor.

It was almost, Sam reckoned, like a small group of them knew more about the Doctor than anyone had realised. Not that Sam was sure how. Or what exactly they were worried by.

'What do you think can go wrong?' That was one of the others, a middle-aged woman in a blue overall.

The Doctor seemed momentarily caught off-guard. Then he shrugged. 'We're in space, and against all that spaceness, this is a very small building with frankly not much between us and out there. All of which is controlled by a computer system that can only be accessed by Chief Hughes. And which, for some reason, UNIT were more than happy to flog off to the first multinational corporation to hit "highest bidder" on eBay. I can already think of eighty-five different scenarios of varying levels of "go wrongness" that make me want to be somewhere else entirely. Oh, and my mate Sam thinks there are space snakes here, too.'

'Snakes on a base?' laughed Hughes. 'There're

no such things as "space snakes"!'

The Doctor held his hands out and shrugged. 'Who knows? But I trust the instincts of a fourteen year old boy over your safety protocols any day.'

'Oh?' said a slightly put-out Christoffel. 'And why's that?'

The Doctor pointed behind them all.

Everyone, and by now absolutely everyone in the room was listening to the Doctor, followed the direction of his pointing finger.

Including Savannah and Sam.

The Doctor was pointing outside, through the big picture window that dominated the far wall.

There, on the dusty surface of the Moon, four shapes slithered towards the base and then reared up, heads flicking back, yellow eyes glinting malevolently.

'Ladies and gentlemen,' said the Doctor quietly, and without any trace of told-you-so in his voice, 'I think those count as space snakes, don't you?'

CHAPTER 9
SEE THE LIGHTS

'Welcome to the Planetarium,' said Commander Cann proudly.

She had led the reduced gang in there after a short walk around the Ring, saying she was taking them somewhere special.

'What about Sam and Savannah?' Caitlin had asked, but Commander Cann said they'd be along in a moment. Although she also looked behind her and grunted in annoyance. 'Well, they should be. I'm sure Chief Llewellyn will chivvy them along.'

The Planetarium was a massive domed room with a ceiling that, according to the Commander, slid open to reveal a screen onto which things could be projected. Apparently it was meant to be an astrophysics guide, so the teams on Moonbase Laika could see how the stars moved and changed over the years. It was able to project images from over five hundred years' of recorded scientific history to map the changes and help predict what might happen in the future.

Commander Cann told the kids that the crew also used it to show 3-D movies from Earth and it was therefore known as the Chill-Out Area – this was where their murals would be painted. Caitlin was especially happy with this.

'But there are no walls,' Hsui said, 'the dome comes right down…'

Commander Cann nodded. 'That's right, so what's the only space to paint on?'

'The inside of the dome itself?' suggested Caitlin.

'Correct. So when people come in here to relax, to chill-out, the entire room, everything they can see, will be covered by your beautiful designs.' The Commander said. 'Except when the dome opens to reveal the projector screen, and it'll all be in the dark then anyway, your paintings will amuse and delight everyone who comes in here.'

'Wow,' breathed Caitlin. 'That is so cool.'

Michael nodded excitedly. 'It is.'

'Want to see something cooler?' asked the Commander. She produced a small remote from a pocket and aimed it at the ceiling, clicking on it as she did so. The inner dome split and started to descend, revealing the massive screen beneath.

A second click and, as the lights went low, a hologram of the solar system appeared on the screen.

'Okay,' said Aaron, nudging Hsui gently. 'Now even I think that's cool.'

Jo Rivas was still standing by the door, frowning.

'Everything okay?' asked her brother, quietly.

'Can you hear that?' she replied.

He listened. 'Nope, what?'

'I thought I could hear a noise.' She crouched down, her hand near the grille of an air vent at the base of the door where it met the floor. 'In here.'

Her brother shrugged. 'Probably just machinery. It's an air vent. Air vents probably pump air. Stop worrying about nothing. I'm more concerned that we can't go home yet, we'll be stuck up here for days. We do have other projects to work on, you know. More important ones that playing nanny to a bunch of geeky kids...'

Jo stopped him. 'Oh, just look at it this way,' she said. 'How often to we get to stand on the Moon?'

'Well, yeah, there is that,' Joe agreed. 'I mean, it is the Moon. That's kind of impressive.'

'Better than taking World State bigwigs around Scunthorpe!' Jo laughed, then stopped. 'There it is again. A hissing.'

She tried to wiggle her fingers through the grille but couldn't get them in. 'Can't feel any air leaking,' she said, relieved. Then gasped.

'What's up?' her brother asked.

Jo pulled her hand back – the tip of one finger was bleeding slightly. 'Must have nicked it on something sharp,' she said, sucking her finger to get the blood off. 'Stupid Moonbase.'

Joe nudged her. 'Doesn't matter, we should probably focus on the Commander. She might be telling the kids about hissing ventilation tubes.'

'Oh, very funny,' his sister said, taking her finger out of her mouth and shaking it.

'Hissss,' he joked.

The look he got in return suggested Jo Rivas wasn't finding her twin very funny at all.

Instead, she went back to listening to Commander Cann.

'Now then,' the Commander was saying, pointing upwards, 'what's that?'

'Mars,' Michael said.

'Good. So if that's Mars and that's Earth and that's Venus, what's that?'

Caitlin turned to Michael, assuming he'd know, but he was silent, turning on his heel, counting the planets displayed above them one after another. Then he did it again. And again. 'That's impossible,' he muttered. 'And more than that, it's silly.'

'Why "silly"?' asked Aaron.

'Because we know all the planets and planetoids

and dwarf-planets and satellites and asteroid fields and… and that's silly.' Michael pointed up at a dull grey ball by Mars, 'that simply shouldn't be there.'

Commander Cann smiled. 'And yet, there it is.'

'Is it a test?' wondered Caitlin. 'To see if brainboxes like him know their stuff?'

Commander Cann shook her head. 'Nope, that's an extrapolation of how the solar system may have looked a few billion years ago. So can you tell me what that planet is?'

Michael shrugged. 'No idea.'

'And none of the experts on Moonbase Laika has either. It popped up some years back when the Hubble Telescope was trained on this area of space for a few days. We know it is very old and no longer exists. Because of the time it takes light to travel, like all things we see in space, it's actually like time travel. We are seeing stars and moons and planets as they were thousands of years ago.'

Michael was so excited. 'Are you saying that Moonbase Laika's mission is to identify and catalogue that new planet? Or I suppose we should say that very old one?'

'Yes, that's one of the things we are doing here.'

Michael was almost beside himself with excitement. 'But why now? Why has no one seen it before? Oh wait, perhaps it's on a weird orbit. If it was in almost perfect alignment with Mars and significantly smaller, and our rotations matched it, it would nearly always be invisible to our telescopes because Mars would be in the way. Maybe it exploded!'

'Why would it do that?' asked Hsui.

'Planets do sometimes, especially if they have molten or ice volcanoes at their core. Maybe it disintegrated millions of years ago. This moon, the moons of Mars and maybe some of the asteroid belt could be the remnants of it.'

For Hsui and presumably all the others this was way beyond them, but they were enjoying Michael's excitement, and finding it infectious.

Commander Cann was nodding, encouraging him, and clearly enjoying swapping thoughts with Michael, challenging him to think. 'Yes, good theory. That is what we are trying to establish. Did the Hubble get a reflection of the past, a unique snapshot of something that universal gravity had kept out of sight for centuries?'

'That's… that's brilliant,' Michael said. 'And exciting. And I want to come and live here and work here and find out!'

Commander Cann grinned. 'And hopefully when you are older, you will, Michael. Because I seriously doubt we'll know the answers in the next decade or so, but hopefully in our lifetime. Maybe we'll find some more mysteries and questions at the same time. It would be boring if we knew everything now. Science is a slow but fantastic art.'

'Where are the others?' asked Caitlin, looking around.

'Other what?' Cann frowned at her. 'There aren't any other planets yet.'

'No. The Rivas twins,' she explained.

Everyone looked around the Planetarium, but the Brand Team were nowhere to be seen.

'Stay here a sec,' Commander Cann sighed,

bringing the lights back up as the dome closed over the screen. 'I'll pop out and find them.' She smiled at the group. 'You see, kids are as good as gold. Pesky adults, can't be left alone for one minute.'

At which moment the loudest, most annoying alarm sounded throughout the base. Commander Cann started for the door, then turned back to the kids. 'Aaron, you're oldest, you're in charge. No one leaves this room till I or one of the Chiefs comes back, okay?'

Aaron nodded. 'Okay.'

And she was gone.

They all stood staring at one another.

'I wonder what that alarm is for,' Michael said, voicing what they were all thinking.

'Nothing good,' Hsui said, moving closer to where the Rivas twins had been standing. 'Alarms never are.'

She was suddenly aware of a strange noise at her feet, down behind the grille – a sort of hissing...

CHAPTER 10
REPULSION

The alarms had sounded because Godfried Christoffel had hit a huge red screen on the wall by the window. A shutter had then closed down over the glass, or whatever glass-substitute it was, blocking everyone's view of the space snakes.

All over the room, and Sam had assumed all over the Moonbase, shutters had come down.

'Emergency protocol Uniform November India Tango,' he shouted and everyone in the room stopped what they were doing and went to different stations.

The lighting in the room dropped to a dull red and it took a few seconds for Sam's eyes to adjust to the changes.

Sam realised the Doctor was at the centre of everything, calmly issuing orders, and getting people motivated. He and Savannah hung back, not wanting to get in the way.

After a few moments, the alarm stopped and Christoffel looked around the room. 'All stations secured. General quarters established. Moonbase Laika is secure and locked down.' From the doorway came Commander Cann's voice, cutting across the room, her tone daring anyone to be anything less than on the ball. She'd obviously hurried back from wherever she had left the others.

'I'm so glad,' she said. 'Now, who wants to tell me why?'

As one, everyone in the room turned expectantly to the Doctor.

'Oh,' he said. 'Oh, you think *I* know? Sorry, no, not really. I mean other than the big space snakes out on the surface of the Moon, I'm not sure what the fuss is about.'

'Space snakes?'

'It's true, Commander,' said Llewellyn Hughes. 'We all saw them.'

'On the surface? The airless surface where nothing can survive.'

'That's right,' said the Doctor. 'Well except for the bits that aren't right. Which would be the "where nothing can survive" line because clearly something can.' He grinned at her. 'Be nice to know how, wouldn't it?'

'It would indeed,' Cann said. 'Godfried?'

The Chief of Security shrugged. 'Never seen anything like them, Commander.'

There was a general murmur in agreement from the rest of the operatives as Cann scanned the room.

'Tell me about the man who warned you.'

After a second, Sam realised the Doctor was talking to him. Slowly, Sam told the brief story of the man he had met and what he'd said.

'Not much to go on,' said Cann. 'A mad old man and a young lad who may or may not be exaggerating.'

'I'm not exaggerating,' said Sam crossly.

'Nevertheless, we need to know what those things are and why they are here now,' said Hughes.

'Oh, they've been here a while I think,' the Doctor said.

'What makes you say that?' asked Cann.

'Well, Sam's old man for starters. And his red box. He said they'd been here before and that would suggest to me that he's probably someone who used to work on this Moonbase,' said the Doctor. 'What do we know about why UNIT built this base?'

'Research into deep space, warning and satellite guidance,' said the older woman Sam had noticed earlier.

'Thank you…?'

'Pauline,' she said. 'Pauline Brown. Medical Station Grade Three.'

'Thank you, Nurse Pauline,' the Doctor smiled. 'Good summation, utterly wrong, but right I suppose if you believe the hype.'

'I'm sorry?' Cann strode across the Area

towards him. 'Lew, can we have the lights back up?'

Immediately the red lighting gave way to the more normal lighting, which seemed to make everyone relax a bit.

'Still on alert,' Christoffel crisply reminded the team. 'There's a bunch of space snakes outside.'

They weren't relaxed any more.

'Why aren't they trying harder to get in?' Hughes asked.

The Doctor shrugged. 'Oh, I imagine they can come and go as they please. Right now, they're just letting us know they are there. Watching. And waiting.'

'For what?' asked Cann.

The Doctor shrugged. 'No idea. But I reckon if they want to get into this base, they wouldn't have much trouble.'

'What do you mean?' Cann was astonished. 'This place is literally airtight. Everyone that comes in or out is recorded, noted. Every change of air pressure, every extra bit of water drunk. No one can just walk through the airlocks and get in here.'

The Doctor threw an arm around Sam and Savannah's shoulders. 'What do you two think? What's the Commander missing in all this?'

Sam looked at Savannah, who shrugged, but then her face lit up. 'They're snakes,' she said.

Sam got it too. 'They don't need to use the doors. They're small and thin.'

Commander Cann still couldn't grasp it. 'What do you mean? There's no other way in.'

The Doctor pointed to the floor. To a grille over the air vents that dotted the room. And every other room and corridor on Moonbase Laika.

'Your air vents are connected by what, tiny thin tunnels, pumping recycled air around on regulated timetables? So, in those downtimes you mentioned earlier, in those areas humans don't go in at night, imagine that something that can live out there, on the surface of the Moon and burrow beneath it isn't going to be stopped by a few plastic tubes,' the Doctor turned to Christoffel. 'I'm guessing that over the last few weeks you've noted unexpected pressure drops, just for a few seconds at a time?

Too brief to register as people coming and going, and so probably ignored – put down to a fault in HEART's systems. But now – now we know what they were. Our little silver friends out there – coming and going.'

Cann stared at Christoffel. 'Chief?'

He shrugged. 'Yeah, tiny drops, just a second here or there. Of course we never gave it much thought. Initially we thought it was a steady leak, but we thoroughly checked that out – there was nothing.'

Commander Cann frowned and pointed at Sam and Savannah as she spoke to Christoffel. 'You didn't tell me? Didn't you think we should cancel these guys' trip if the base wasn't 101% safe?'

'I bet he did. He's a good Chief of Security,' smiled the Doctor. 'I bet that's exactly what you did. Rather than worry the Commander over something so trivial, I bet you mentioned it to someone in engineering design at World State, got them to check the schematics first, am I right?'

'I did. Word came back that World State thought

it would be bad PR to cancel.'

'Really? I wonder why… ah! Of course, I should have realised earlier. Aaron Relevy – he has a camera mounted on his baseball cap.' He turned to Sam and Savannah. 'Permanently recording everything?'

Sam reckoned so. 'Probably sends a feed back to Earth, too.'

'Unless the snakes want to be seen,' he murmured. 'I wonder if they're receiving now.' The Doctor let this all sink in. 'They are clever and cunning,' he said. 'There's a lot of intelligence in those snakes. They want to be seen. Otherwise, why say hello just now?'

'I don't understand,' said Savannah.

'Of course you don't,' smiled the Doctor 'Why should you? At your age you should be thinking about ponies and pop music and fashion and how to date boys like Sam here.' He stopped and looked at Sam. 'Well, she should!' he carried on,.'No, Savannah, you shouldn't have to worry that when UNIT was set up back in the 1970s, it needed places to store things that it found, strange alien things that it won in battle. Over the years they stored stuff in a variety of places – vaults, forges, Torchwoods even. But at the turn of the century, they built themselves a nice little Moonbase up here, not to keep a safe eye on Earth (although I'm sure it helped) but somewhere safe to store stuff. Space viruses; plastic eating nanites from Phophov IV – oh, that was a battle and a half, believe me, it's why the CD industry had to give way to MP3 downloads – plus guns, tanks and other assorted weapons too dangerous to leave on Earth. Then there's a Hopkiss Diamond – I had such fun vibrating that to communicate with its owners back on Jool. On their planet, "Doctor" translated as "Jeweller" – Jeweller to the Stars they named me. I like that. So much less aggressive than "the Oncoming Storm" or "Destroyer of Worlds" or "Bow tie of Doom". No one has ever really called me that, by the way. Bow ties are never doom-y. Well, rarely.' The Doctor spun around and looked straight at Sam and Savannah. 'Oh, oh I wonder if the RavnoPortal Beast of Birodonne is still locked away here. Now him you'd love to see. All he ever wanted to do was eat up little... no, no perhaps you don't want to meet him actually. Bad move. Bad RavnoPortal Beast of Birodonne. Baaaad.'

He addressed the Commander again. 'So, that's the question. What happened to everything UNIT used to have back up here – before World State so mysteriously bought this place up? Did they take it somewhere else, or did they leave it here? Did World State inherit a nice empty Moonbase, or did it come with a literal arsenal of lethal lethalness? And if so, why? We're a few decades off war, the Oil Apocalypse and the intellectual copyright battle between T-Mat and iTeleport. Lots of questions and no answers.'

'UNIT took everything as far as we know,' Christoffel said. 'World State inherited nothing.'

'Well except for our serpentine chums,' said the Doctor. And then, suddenly, he held up a hand. 'Shhhh. Listen.'

And everyone did so.

They could hear a tiny scrabbling sound, a faint hissing.

The Doctor pointed to one of the vents. Then another. And another.

'We have visitors,' he said. 'I'm not sure we should invite them in…'

CHAPTER 11
MONSTER

Back in the Planetarium, Hsui told Aaron about the hissing she'd heard from below.

'Machinery?' she wondered.

'The projection equipment?' he suggested.

'A leak? Are we losing air?' Michael said, earning himself a thump on the arm from Caitlin.

They had been warned about this more than anything in their training back on Earth. Of all the trials and tribulations that faced people living on Moonbase Laika, the ever-present threat of decompression was the most important to be aware of. Even the smallest hole, smaller than a pinprick, could kill everyone in seconds.

'We are *not* losing air,' Caitlin said.

'Well, actually…' started Michael, until Caitlin cut him off again.

'We. Are. Not. Losing. Air. All right?' she said, in a manner that dared Michael to argue.

He didn't.

It was then that they heard more sounds – slithering and sliding noises, which definitely seemed to come from beneath them.

Aaron took charge. He remembered what they had been told during an emergency drill situation, when training for this trip.

'Sit down,' said Aaron. 'Like they taught us, in a circle.'

And everyone did. 'Is everyone okay?' Aaron asked.

One by one they answered they were okay, if a bit nervous.

'We stay here as long as possible as the Commander asked. We don't leave the Planetarium until someone comes back to find us. Or unless we really need to. Basically, if something has gone wrong, this may be the safest place to be.'

'What makes you say that?' Hsui asked.

'Because we're not dead yet,' Aaron replied grimly.

Suddenly, there was a massive hissing from beneath them, and everyone cried out in surprise as all the vent grilles, about six of them, flew away from the walls, as if massive pressure had been pushed against them.

'Everyone, get closer. Take someone's hand,' Aaron ordered.

'I'm not holding Caitlin's hand,' yelled Michael.

'You are now,' Caitlin replied. 'Grow up!'

Aaron grabbed Hsui's hand and squeezed it tightly. 'Form a chain,' he shouted. 'We are stronger and safer if we are one.'

'Not necessarily,' Michael muttered. 'If the place has sprung a leak, we all get dragged out into space together if we're holding hands.'

'Not helping,' Aaron said.

'Just saying…'

Suddenly the room was filled with flashes of silver!

Hsui screamed and Michael yelled.

Snakes!

The floor was swarming with slithering silver snakes, dashing about, rearing up and hissing at everyone.

Aaron's camera on his cap recorded it all – the snakes raring up, spreading their hoods, dark yellow eyes glinting. The yells and cries of the gang, Aaron trying to keep them together, to protect each other, and slowly trying to find a way towards the door. He lead the gang bravely, but with each turn they took, more snakes blocked their path.

After a few minutes, Aaron told them to stand still.

'They aren't attacking us!' he shouted.

'Yet,' Michael added.

But Caitlin could see what Aaron meant. 'They had a chance to, but they're not. They're just… just…'

'Herding us,' Aaron said slowly, realising that they were now standing right at the centre of the room.

The snakes stopped moving but never took their eyes off the gang.

'Why?' asked Hsui. 'Why don't they attack?'

Michael took a deep breath, trying to push down his fear and start thinking rationally, like the scientist Commander Cann had suggested he might one day be.

'They want something,' he said. 'But not from us.'

'They are waiting,' Aaron agreed.

The Planetarium door swung open and Godfried Christoffel rushed in with some of his men. In their hands they clutched fire extinguishers, which they activated, spraying the snakes with CO_2 foam.

The snakes moved fast, but not towards any of the humans. Back, back the way they had come, into the vent tubes that lined the underside of the Moonbase.

Immediately everyone leapt forward with questions, but Christoffel shushed them. 'Let's get you back to the others,' he said and his men led the shaken but no longer scared gang away.

'Whose idea was sticking together, holding hands, forming a chain?' Christoffel asked them as they headed out.

'Aaron's,' Hsui said proudly.

'Good call,' Christoffel said. 'Most people wouldn't think that quickly. Well done.'

Hsui was convinced Aaron grew a couple of inches in pride at that.

CHAPTER 12
HUNTER AND THE HUNTED

Christoffel led them into another room, a laboratory, called the Shaw Labs.

It smelled sterile and unwelcoming, but the gang were relieved to see Sam, Savannah and the Doctor there, setting out comfortable chairs, and waving to each of them to sit.

Commander Cann was talking to the people there, most of whom were from the Command Area.

'Moonbase Laika is on lockdown. The crew have locked themselves either in their cabins or in the Mess Area. I have activated Emergency Code Alpha – so the only people with roaming privileges around the Moonbase are the people in this room. That way, I know where everyone is. Moonbase Laika is secure.'

'Apart from the Space Snakes,' said Hsui.

'They were all over the Planetarium, Commander,' explained Christoffel. 'We fought them off, they went back into the vents.'

The Commander blew air out of her cheeks. 'Doctor?'

'When they built Moonbase Laika,' the Doctor was saying as he bustled around, 'they built it to withstand... well, a lot. UNIT were good like that, being militaristic, they tend to make everything as impregnable as possible.'

'Could a nuclear warhead take it out?' Sam asked.

The Doctor gave him a look that suggested probably not, but he didn't actually answer, instead he waved an arm around the lab. 'This is the most well-protected room other than HEART according to Chief Hughes. Which makes sense because labs on Moonbases are never the safest areas, all those experiments and stuff that can go

"BOOM" at inconvenient times. It's best to make sure nothing external can get in and, in the event of chemical fires or whatever, nothing can get out.'

'And yes, just for the record, a nuclear warhead could destroy this place. So could the nuclear power core that makes it all work,' Commander Cann added.

Chief Hughes nodded. 'In the event of an emergency, from within HEART I can destroy —'

The Doctor put his fingers to his lips, making a shushing sound. 'I don't think our young artists need to know about that,' he said.

The Chief of Science nodded and sat down.

The Doctor smiled at all of them, visitors and staff alike. 'So, I imagine you're wondering why I've asked you here. Oh, always wanted to say that. I sound like a proper academic.'

'Snakes?' suggested Michael.

'Indeed. Out there, on the surface, something is alive and Space Snakes seems to be a good description.'

'Scary metal ones.' That was Caitlin.

'Metal?' asked Savannah.

'Yeah, close up, it looked like they were made of metal,' Caitlin replied.

'So a potentially interesting life form, if you think about it.' The Doctor was up again, walking around. 'Reptilian life forms enhanced by some kind of living metal, maybe some kind of nano-technology, maybe some kind of robot.'

'Or,' said Michael, 'snakes in spacesuits.'

Caitlin sniggered, despite her fear.

But the Doctor had stopped and was looking squarely at Michael. Then he glanced up to Hughes, Christoffel and the Commander.

'That, young man, is brilliant.' The Doctor was now standing by Hughes. 'We simply didn't consider that – snakes in spacesuits. We need suits to live on or under the Moon, why shouldn't they?'

'Because they are snakes?' Hughes suggested. 'Alien snakes. That have just swarmed through this base.'

'In spacesuits,' added Michael.

'Well, they've swarmed over one specific part

of it, the Planetarium,' said Aaron.

'Were they actually doing anything other than slithering around?' asked the Doctor.

Aaron shrugged. 'Probably – I wasn't really thinking about that.'

'No,' said the Doctor calmly, placing a hand on Aaron's shoulder. 'No, of course you weren't. You were saving everyone else's lives. Which is exactly what you should have done.' And he turned to look at Aaron. 'So thank you.'

'What for?' Aaron asked.

'Being brave. And brilliant.' He swung back to the others. 'So, why swarm into the Planetarium, the "chill-out area" as I believe you call it? What's in there of all places? I mean they can get through the vent tubes, which gives them access to everywhere on Moonbase Laika, so why go somewhere so insignificant? Command Area? No. These labs? No. Living quarters? Food halls? Nope, just the big shiny recreation room.'

'Perhaps they wanted to watch a movie,' Caitlin said, remembering what Commander Cann had said before.

'Not likely,' the Commander muttered.

'Or,' said Michael slowly, 'perhaps they wanted to see something else.'

Hsui clapped her hands. 'The planets, the stars. We were looking at those before the alarm started…'

'When we saw the snakes outside on the surface,' Savannah added.

'As a distraction,' Sam added. 'We were busy worrying about them, giving others time to get into the Planetarium.'

'Absolutely,' the Doctor agreed. 'Clever snakes in spacesuits. Oh, I love you kids. You all think outside the box. Brilliant. You are all brilliant. Be more brilliant – why would you want to see the solar system? I mean it's pretty and all that, but hardly unique.'

'What about that strange planet, the one we didn't know whether it was old or new?' Michael said to the Commander.

'Oooh, what new/old planet?' asked the

Doctor, and Commander Cann repeated to him what she had told the others.

'And the Rivas twins?' asked Hsui.

'Oh yes, where are they?' The Doctor looked around the room as if he'd only just noticed they were missing. He even looked under a bench. 'Not really very likely, is it, Doctor,' he muttered to himself. 'You'd see them hiding under a bench. Gotta think straight.'

'They wandered off, and I couldn't find them anywhere,' Commander Cann said. She turned to Christoffel. 'Chief, you better get some people out looking for them.'

The Doctor held a hand up. 'Hang on,' he looked at Christoffel. 'Anyone else gone missing recently?'

Christoffel tried not to glance at his Commander, but everyone noticed.

'I'll take that as a yes,' the Doctor said.

'Not exactly,' said the Commander with a sigh. 'This is so not my best day,' she muttered. 'Over the last couple of weeks, a number of staff have gone missing for a short space of time but we always find them eventually, usually in their cabins. They have no memory of how they got there or anything.'

The Doctor turned to Pauline Brown. 'Nurse Pauline?'

She shrugged. 'Our best guess at first was some kind of electric shock they were getting, creating temporary amnesia. But we had no real answers.'

The Doctor smiled grimly at the Commander. 'Amnesiac staff. Power losses. Space Snakes in silver spacesuits. You're right, it's just not your day is it?'

'Thank you,' the Commander said. 'Anything useful to add?'

'When was the last case, Nurse Pauline?'

She glanced at Llewellyn Hughes. 'This morning, wasn't it? Sym?'

The Chief nodded in agreement. 'One of my staff, doing routines in HEART, found himself in the Mess shortly before you lot arrived.'

The Commander suddenly looked at the

Doctor.

'Oh, don't give me that "Oh, so it's all your fault" look, Commander, that gets boring very quickly, with all the questions and the "Where were you when A happened to B". Trust me, it's nothing to do with me.'

'Oh great,' the Commander drawled. '"Trust me" he says. Like I have any choice.'

'Can't the big computer help us?' the Doctor asked. 'See if it can find any links between the disappearances, the power losses and the arrival of the Outer Space Reptile Race?'

Chief Hughes nodded 'I'll go program the variables into HEART and see what it can suggest.'

'If HEART could scan under the Moon's surface,' Michael suggested, 'that might tell us where the Space Snakes are.'

'I like him,' the Doctor said. 'A lot. Chief?'

Hughes nodded, 'Worth a try.' The Welshman looked at Michael. 'Want to come with me?'

Michael was standing beside him faster than the others could blink!

'Stay in contact please,' the Doctor requested.

Christoffel opened a drawer, took out some headsets and tossed them to Hughes.

'Thanks,' Hughes said and fitted one to Michael and then to himself. 'We'll talk you through everything,' he said.

Christoffel activated a large widescreen monitor built into the wall and a split image of thin green lines, one above the other, appeared. 'Speak,' he said to Michael.

'What should I say… oh cool!'

On the screen as he'd spoken, the green line became a waveform.

When Hughes spoke, the upper line did the same. 'It's two way, Doctor. You just speak aloud and we can hear you.'

'Magic,' the Doctor said.

'Science,' said Michael grinning at him.

'Get outta here,' the Doctor laughed. 'And Chief?'

'Doctor?'

'Be careful. Both of you. We lost the Rivas

Twins. I don't want to lose you two too.'

'We'll be fine.'

He and Michael left the lab.

The Doctor turned to Aaron. 'Mr Relevy?'

'Doctor?'

'You've been in showbusiness a while, right? Tell me about the camera on your cap.'

'Records via a bluetooth to a hard-drive in my luggage. Broadcast quality digital visual transmissions to Earth from up here are still a bit in the future.'

'So my question is, is anything you see here being transmitted back to World State right now?'

'No.'

Sam looked at him. 'But I thought…?'

'It's a fake, a lie.' Aaron said. 'Of sorts. I mean, the footage will end up on Earth and will be shown, but it's just being recorded and stored for now. I'm meant to upload a package each night and then transmit it back. They'll edit and broadcast.'

'But everyone on Earth thinks they're seeing real time broadcasts?'

'Everyone knows there's a time delay – it's like the old Big Brother live feeds from twenty years ago, everyone knows it's not really live. But in this case, the delay is more than a few moments. Just in case…'

'In case what?' asked Savannah.

'In case it all goes wrong,' said Sam quietly. 'And we all die.'

'Die?' said an alarmed Caitlin. 'They said everything was safe up here. World State never warned us about Space Snakes…'

'Well, good,' the Doctor cut across her. 'Your *BPXtra* is going to witness a peaceful encounter with charming space snakes in spacesuits,' he smiled. 'Back in the Planetarium, I presume you got the whole thing on camera?'

Aaron nodded. 'I guess so, yeah, must've.'

The Doctor threw an arm around his shoulder. 'Never stop recording, Mr Relevy. It could be very important, historically speaking – it seems our clever old snakes want witnesses to the history being made up here.'

'Doctor?' Nurse Pauline indicated the readings coming from the speaker sets worn by Hughes and Michael.

'Can you hear us, Doctor?' asked Michael. The green line wavered and changed in rhythm with his voice.

'Absolutely, Michael. Where are you?'

'We're outside HEART,' Chief Hughes said.

'The Chief is entering the access codes so we can get in.' Michael sounded excited and the green lines bounced up and down even more, as if to underline this.

There was a few seconds of silence.

'Guys?' said Commander Cann. There was no response.

'What's going on?' Sam asked but the Doctor hushed him.

More seconds of silence, although they could hear both people breathing, the effect on the waveforms was slight but reassuring.

The waveforms fluctuated at the noise of a door opening, a complicated sounding series of clicks and whirrs as, presumably, lots of small parts opened, one at a time.

Sam looked around the room. Various people in coloured coveralls looking concerned, including Pauline and Christoffel. They were the only Moonbase staff not locked safely in their cabins, all being brave together during the emergency.

The Doctor stood completely still, eyes tightly closed, listening intently.

Caitlin had sat on her hands to stop herself fidgeting, clearly trying her best not to be scared.

And Savannah stared at the Doctor, as if hoping he would have all the answers.

Sam was convinced he already had. He had faith in the mysterious Doctor.

Next to Hsui was Aaron, whose hand slipped casually into hers and gripped tightly.

She gripped back.

Still nothing.

'Chief?' the Doctor said suddenly. 'Report?' His eyes snapped open.

Nothing.

'Lew?' Christoffel asked.

'Michael?' Savannah tried.

Nothing.

The waveforms were straight lines.

No sound. Not even breathing.

It was as if Michael and the Chief of Science had simply vanished.

CHAPTER 13
BULLETPROOF
HEART

Realising that they had lost contact with Llewellyn Hughes and Micheal Griffin, the Doctor and Godfried Christoffel came up with another plan.

It sounded equally insane, Sam reckoned.

'We'll go after them, retrace their steps,' said Christoffel.

'Um, no you won't,' said Commander Cann.

'Look, Plan A failed, and I'm feeling rather responsible for that,' the Doctor snapped at her. 'And very responsible for Chief Hughes and young Michael. So Plan B it is.'

Christoffel argued, 'First we have to know —'

'We do know,' snapped the Commander. 'Either

the snakes didn't want them getting into HEART, or they've taken them over to do something specific – which implies that the snakes can't actually get into HEART itself. Maybe the energy it gives off repels them....'

The Doctor was making a gesture with his arm, wriggling it, doing a pretending-to-be-a-snake thing, but in silence. Then he pointed straight up, into the ceiling and made a mime that was about long tubes and tunnels and he did more arm wriggling.

Sam realised he meant that the snakes were inside the base, within the slender tubes that contained the power cables threaded throughout the ceilings and floors of the base. A perfect way to get around without being detected.

The Doctor put his hand to his ear and again did the arm wriggling gesture. He meant the snakes had overheard their conversations!

Sam watched as the Doctor finished his mime. He slowed, stopped, as he, and Sam himself, became aware that everyone in the lab had stopped watching him and were now looking behind them.

To the doorway.

Standing there was a group of people.

Llewellyn Hughes. Michael Griffin. The Rivas twins.

'Hullo,' said the Doctor. 'Love people who know how to make an entrance.'

'I want to go home,' said Michael.

'Well, obviously,' said the Doctor. 'But I'm not sure that right now we can –'

'I want to go home,' said Jo Rivas.

'Home is important,' said Joe.

'I'm sensing a theme,' said the Doctor.

'It couldn't be located,' said Hughes. 'Where is the red box?'

'They've been taken over by the Space Snakes!' said Caitlin.

'Haven't they just?' the Doctor murmured, wandering towards the newcomers. 'Bite marks on the hands, certainly.' He waved a hand in front of Hughes's face, but got no reaction. 'Hullo?'

'We have to leave,' said Michael. 'Now. Go home.'

The Doctor stepped back. 'I think we got the message. May I ask a question?'

All of them said "Yes" at the same time, their heads turning in unison, like puppets being controlled simultaneously.

The Doctor held his hands out. 'Are you responsible for the power losses? The crew getting amnesia?'

'Yes,' the four chorused in that same eerie way.

'Why?' Commander Cann asked

'We were… investigating your base,' replied Joe Rivas alone. 'We want the red box.'

The Doctor paused, just for a brief second, then burst into a jumble of hand waving and walking in circles. 'Of course,' he said. 'Remember I said this used to be a UNIT base, full of weapons and alien artefacts and stuff? Well, the snakes are knocking on your door, politely. Sort of politely anyway. Trying to ask for help.'

'Help?' said Commander Cann.

'Yup, Commander. These are aliens, yeah? Aliens who want something UNIT took, something you,

World State, whoever, inherited. "Can I have my ball back please?" That sort of thing. Except "ball" could mean utterly lethal thermonuclear warhead, or huge vial of devastating bubonic outer space plague or perhaps even the massive RavnoPortal Beast of Birodonne.' The Doctor turned back to the mesmerised group. 'So, you don't want to hurt anyone, but you make people want to go home. That makes you rather antisocial Space Snakes in spacesuits. Tell you what, why don't you talk to me directly rather than through intermediaries. I get very bored talking to monkeys when the organ-grinder isn't far away. Don't want to talk to the handymen when the gaffer is... anyway, I think you get my point.'

He stood, waiting. Perhaps expecting a snake (hopefully not a hundred) to flop out of the ceiling to have a chat.

It didn't happen.

'Well, that was an anticlimax,' the Doctor said.

He pushed past the possessed people and into the corridor. 'Plan B again, Mr Christoffel. Which way to HEART please?'

The Commander was with him in a second. 'Again, I don't think that's wise. I don't think I can afford to risk losing you too, Doctor.'

'Very flattering, yes and you're right, you probably can't to afford to lose me because without me, no one's going to get through to the snakes, find out what's going on and free the minds of those four people.' He poked Commander Cann's shoulder. 'I'm pretty magnificent really and that's why I want to keep on the move. If I stay around here, they might start making more and more hostages out of you lot and I'll achieve nothing. This way, I may learn something useful with which to negotiate.'

Sam and Savannah had followed them to the door of the laboratory. 'Do you need anyone to come with you?'

The Doctor thought about this. 'Savannah, I want you two to see if you can help the Commander find anything, anything in the records of this place that might help us work out what they want.'

'They want a box,' Aaron called out.

'Lot of boxes on a Moonbase like this,' the Commander said.

'Any red ones?' Hsui wondered.

'We should also consider why they took the Rivas Twins,' the Doctor said. 'What do they want with them?'

'Hostages?' suggested Christoffel.

The Doctor shook his head. 'Everything they've done has had a reason, nothing has been random.' He turned to Aaron and Hsui. 'World State, they represent World State. Maybe it's something to do with that. Can you remember either of them carrying any red World State boxes?'

'I don't think so,' Hsui said. 'I didn't see them with anything like that.'

'Their smartphones,' Aaron said, thinking aloud. 'They were always on them – if they have anything on any of us, I bet it'll be stored on their phones.'

'Password protected, I bet,' said Hsui. 'They seem the type to be security-minded.'

Aaron walked over to where the four people were standing, motionless. Almost as if they had been switched off.

Aaron reached into both Rivas's pockets and took out their smartphones. 'Easy,' he said.

'Now what?' asked Hsui.

Aaron smiled. 'I'm a man who builds top of the range tech from scrap metal. Getting past a few encrypted passwords should be a doddle,' he smiled. 'And those two are unlikely to use anything too complicated in case they need to access one another's phones in an emergency. Give me ten minutes with a computer on this base and I can sort it.'

'Good man,' said the Doctor. 'You do that, Caitlin, look after Michael and the others. Can you do that for me?'

Caitlin swallowed hard, then said, 'Of course, Doctor.'

'Thank you,' and he winked at her. 'And Chief Christoffel?'

'Doctor?'

'The snakes are coming in through the vent grilles. Might be worth a round of blocking them up for now, just till we get this sorted?'

Christoffel sighed. 'And if we don't?'

'Then perhaps the snakes will have killed us long before we run out of clean air,' said Commander Cann.

'Oh, if the snakes wanted us dead,' the Doctor said, 'they could have smashed in the windows and sucked us all to our doom ages ago. No, I'm not getting hostility from them – they didn't hurt the guys in the Planetarium or anyone they've knocked out. No, no they need us alive and kicking.'

'Okay,' said Commander Cann. 'Heaven knows why, but I'm placing the safety of Moonbase Laika in your hands, Doctor. Don't get us all killed. Please.'

He smiled at her. 'I'll try not to.' He then nudged Sam. 'Well Mr Miller?'

'Yes, Doctor?'

'Come with me?'

'Absolutely,' Sam grinned.

Together they wandered off down the corridor, talking all the time.

'Are you scared, Sam?'

'A little,' Sam confessed. 'But it seems kind of okay when you're around.'

The Doctor smiled. 'Glad to hear you say that. Now let's consider what we know. Snakes on a base. Searching for a box. Been everywhere they can. Can't find it.'

'Apparently they saw something in the Planetarium,' offered Sam.

'True, true – but what? Should we pop in there, see if there's anywhere to hide a red box?'

Sam thought about it then said no. 'The others were there and someone like Aaron would remember if there was a red box – he's quite sharp.'

'He is indeed,' the Doctor agreed. 'So let's forget the Planetarium for now. Which brings us back to our current destination.'

'HEART?'

'HEART indeed. I think the Commander is correct – the snakes keep taking over people who work in there, but they clearly can't go inside themselves. The energies it gives off can't be good for them.'

Sam was counting the facts off on his fingers. 'So if the red box is inside HEART, how come no one has ever seen it?'

The Doctor clapped his hands. 'Red box! Of course, *I've* seen the red box!'

'Where?' asked Sam.

'Ten years ago, out on the surface of the Moon. Lukas Minski – lovely man, bit preoccupied I reckon. I thought I saw something move but he dismissed it. But what if he encountered the snakes right then? What if it's *his* red toolbox we're looking for?'

Sam nodded caught up in the Doctor's enthusiasm. 'So... so what's inside the box?' he asked.

'Not. A. Clue.' The Doctor stopped walking and closed his eyes, probably trying to picture what he saw ten years ago, Sam reckoned. 'Nope, nothing. But I have something the snakes don't,' he added as he started walking again. 'My secret weapon, if you like.'

'A gun?'

'Okay, not a weapon. Bad choice of words. Infinitely better than anything as yukky as a gun.'

'What is it then?' Sam wondered.

But the Doctor just winked and said nothing else until they reached HEART.

The door was open, revealing the glowing interior, just as Hughes and Michael had left it when they were taken over by the Space Snakes.

Taking a deep breath, the Doctor walked in.

'Is it safe?' Sam asked.

'Unless you're an Outer Space Space Snake, absolutely,' the Doctor waved him inside.

Sam looked around HEART. The walls glowed with a variety of different colours, as if HEART was alive, breathing. Beating silently.

It was warm. It smelled... odd.

'It's electrical.' The Doctor licked his finger and held it up. 'Supercharging the air. That's probably what can't be good for our reptile chums.'

'It's like just before a storm hits,' Sam said.

They looked around the HEART chamber. It was no larger than an average living room, but it was like a cylinder that went up quite a long way. Sam couldn't actually see the top because the flashing lights made everything up there too hazy to focus on. 'Wow,' he said. 'This is amazing.'

A series of small ladders were fixed to the wall and, like Sym Sergei had done some hours earlier, the Doctor started climbing up into the heart of HEART.

'Everything on Moonbase Laika is controlled from here,' he called down to Sam. 'Everything. That's an incredible feat of engineering. And a bit stupid.'

'Why stupid?'

'Well obviously it's stupid. I mean, sabotage this place and you wipe out the base.'

'More proof the snakes want us alive then,' Sam said. 'If they took over the people that control this, like Chief Hughes, they could have killed us easily.'

'I like the way you think, Sam,' the Doctor said, waving his hand through the air. 'And now it's secret weapon time.'

The Doctor produced something from his inside pocket. It looked like a big pen or thin torch, and it made a buzzing sound and glowed green as he ran it over a number of HEART's glowing panels.

'What is it?' Sam asked.

'Say hullo to my Sonic Screwdriver,' the Doctor said. 'An app for every occasion. Except wood. And water. And it's not hot yet on deadlock seals. But a good old microstate seal like this – easy-peasy lemon squeezy.' Sudddenly one of the panels stopped glowing and dropped forward. The Doctor reached inside, and then smiled. 'Gotcha. Oh, Lukas Minski, you clever man.'

He pulled out a red toolbox.

Sam grinned 'How did you know where to find it?'

'Set the Sonic to find an irregular energy pulse, because I guessed Lukas had hidden it where no one would look, and it was just blocking enough of the energy for the Sonic to notice, but not enough for Moonbase Laika's less sophisticated instruments to detect.'

Sam was startled. '"Less sophisticated"? But this place is state-of-the-art...'

The Doctor switched off his Sonic Screwdriver. 'And my little Sonic here makes this Moonbase look like a prehistoric cave dwelling.' He patted one of HEART's panels. 'No disrespect intended.'

He jumped down and passed the red toolbox to Sam. 'Please can you take this, I may have my arms metaphorically full when we get back to the lab and chat to the snakes.'

'Why?' asked Sam.

The Doctor shrugged. 'Because they want it back.'

'So can't we give it to them?' asked Sam.

The Doctor paused. 'Maybe. Maybe not. I rather want to know what is in it before I give it back to them. They've not exactly been up-front about this, and there's a lot of biting been going on. I don't like bitey things as a rule.'

A new thought crossed Sam's mind, and he looked at the red box. 'It's not a bomb is it?'

The Doctor stopped. 'Ooh. Ooh I hadn't considered that. Maybe it is.'

'Sam frowned. 'Great. I'm carrying a bomb.'

'Well, we better get it away from all this energy flying about in HEART then.' The Doctor strode off. 'Come along, Sam. Time to talk to the snakes.'

CHAPTER 14
BANGING ON THE DOOR

Hsui, Caitlin and Savannah were grouped around Michael. The Rivas twins and Chief Hughes were stood slightly apart, but that was because they had moved as the trio gathered around their friend.

'Michael?' Caitlin said quietly. 'Michael can you hear us?'

'I want to go home,' said Michael dully. He was just repeating it over and over again, as if it was the only thing he could say.

'We all do,' Savannah said.

And then it hit Caitlin – something the Doctor had said, about the whole "going home" thing.

'Got it!' she said rather loudly.

Everyone in the laboratory stopped whatever they were doing.

'What do you mean, Caitlin?' asked Commander Cann.

Caitlin took a breath. She didn't want to muck this up, in case no one took her seriously. She wondered how the Doctor would get this across to everyone. All these experienced people living on the Moon, living in space and here she was, eleven years old and maybe about to solve a mystery.

Or make a fool of herself.

Here goes nothing, she thought.

'It's not Michael and the others who want to go home,' she started. 'The Space Snakes are talking through them, yes? So it's them. The snakes are telling us *they* want to go home.'

'Where is home?' the Commander wondered.

'That planet,' said Caitlin. 'The mysterious one you and Michael were talking about earlier, in the Planetarium. That's why they swarmed in there, they wanted us to see that planet but we'd already switched it off.' Caitlin smiled. It made sense to her anyway.

Commander Cann grinned. 'You know what guys, as theories go, I've not heard a better one.'

Caitlin almost blushed with pride at that. She'd been right to speak up.

'And you won't hear a better one,' said a voice from the door.

'Doctor!'

'Because Caitlin is utterly correct,' the Doctor finished, as he carefully closed the laboratory door behind him. 'Well, I don't know about the planet obviously 'cos I haven't seen that but it sounds plausible.'

Sam was holding the box out carefully. Old, red and metallic, like the strange old man had said.

'You found it?' Chief Christoffel said. 'What is it?'

'Hopefully not a bomb,' Sam muttered.

'You know what, I reckon it's just a box, Sam,' the Doctor said, gently.

Sam wanted to feel convinced, but he wasn't entirely. 'That man I met on Earth mentioned this box to me. And he warned me about the snakes. Why did he tell *me*?'

'Wrong place, wrong time,' the Doctor said gently. 'Could have been any of you who saw that man, but it was you. Tell us again what happened.'

'He walked over, knelt down and warned me about the snakes, told me to look out for a red box and said goodbye.'

'Anything else?' prompted Commander Cann.

'We shook hands.' Sam remembered. 'Oh. Oh and he said something weird as he left.'

'Yes?' the Doctor encouraged.

Sam frowned. 'I wasn't really listening at the time, but now it seems appropriate. He said something about it being time to go home.'

The Doctor nodded.

'But if the snakes want the box,' asked Caitlin. 'why didn't they get it themselves?'

Savannah laughed for the first time in ages. Sam thought it was a nice sound. 'They're snakes,' she said. 'No hands – how could they carry it from where Sam found it?'

She smiled at him, proudly. Sam was about to say that strictly speaking the Doctor had found it, but the Doctor nudged him. 'He was brilliant, Savannah. I'm very proud of him.'

Sam was delighted to see Savannah grin more broadly. And this time, Sam didn't blush.

'Talking of which – where was it?' asked Christoffel. 'I mean, I have no idea what's going on here, but it seems a reasonable question.'

'Inside HEART, locked away in a safe place all those years ago. Where the power and energy in HEART would keep whatever is inside it safe I imagine,' the Doctor said. 'And because of the energies inside HEART, they couldn't go in and get it themselves. Well, and as Savannah said so brilliantly, how were they going to get it out anyway? They needed someone human to do that.'

'So why you?' asked Caitlin.

'Oh, it's not really about me,' the Doctor smiled. 'But a few years back, I was standing in a spacesuit, next to a man called Lukas Minski, when I saw him open it. So I can at least remember the access code.'

'You were there?' asked Commander Cann. 'Then where is he now? He needs to explain why he put it in HEART.'

'He's on Earth,' said Sam. 'That's the man I saw, wasn't it Doctor?'

Aaron was more concerned with the snakes. 'Okay, but why are they here? What do they want now?'

'Remember what I said earlier, Aaron? To lovely Pauline over there, about aliens turning up and asking for their ball back? I think these guys want their metaphorical ball back – whatever it is, it's been locked inside a red metal toolbox for the past decade.'

'Are you sure they should have it?' asked Hsui.

Suddenly, there was a terrible noise, like a massive hammering on the doors of the laboratory. And the walls. And the floors.

'Snakes,' said Christoffel.

'Space Snakes, in spacesuits,' added Savannah.

'Space Snakes in spacesuits who would very much like to come in and get whatever's in the box, I reckon,' said the Doctor.

'Should we let them in?' asked Caitlin.

'Oh yes,' said the Doctor. 'I think it's time we finished this little mystery once and for all.'

He crossed to the door, turned the handle and let them in.

CHAPTER 15
STARS WILL LEAD THE WAY

Godfried Christoffel and the rest of the Moonbase Laika staff, even Pauline Brown, formed a protective circle around the children and the other visitors.

'They aren't going to hurt anyone,' the Doctor said, loudly enough for everyone to hear. 'Because if they do, they'll annoy me. And that's their only bargaining chip gone. Unhappy Doctor means they don't get inside this box.'

Sam was astonished to see the snakes actually slither backwards slightly.

He stared at them in horrified fascination. He could see, now he was right up close to them and not running away, they were indeed, just as Michael had suggested earlier, wearing silver spacesuits – clearly designed to survive in zero gravity, and transparent globes covered their cobra-like heads, some of which were open, presumably allowing the snakes' jaws to bite anyone if they felt the need. Other than that, they were normal snake-sized, sleek, shiny and very hostile-looking. Their eyes glowed a fierce luminous yellow, their heads swayed from side to side as if sizing up their enemies.

Sam hoped they weren't getting ready to rip everyone's throats out.

The Doctor took the red toolbox from him and slowly turned to face the Space Snakes.

Sam heard him make some very strange noises, which seemed to come deep from within his throat. They weren't words, they were noises, breaths, staccato-style, but deep and quite scary. For a second, Sam wondered if the snakes had somehow taken him over too, but he seemed fine.

The snakes however, backed even further away,

except one, which came closer to the Doctor, reared up and spread its cobra-like canopy even further.

The leader, Sam guessed.

And then it made similar sounds back at the Doctor.

'Absolutely,' the Doctor said normally again. 'And I'm afraid it hurts my throat to do it, so I'd prefer to speak English, if that's okay?'

The snake made another guttural hiss.

Sam and the others just stared at the Doctor.

'You speak snake?' called Caitlin. 'Are you like Harry Potter?'

'No,' the Doctor said. 'But I do speak Outer Space Alien Snake. And I'm very different from Harry Potter – although I did get locked in a cupboard under the stairs when I was your age by my uncle.'

'Cool.'

'Not especially. But I had been very naughty and deserved it.'

'Doctor!' That was Commander Cann.

'Yes?'

'Space Snakes? Danger? Mesmerised people?'

'Oh yeah, sorry,' the Doctor shrugged. He offered the box towards the Leader Snake. 'You want this, but there are terms.'

The Leader Snake hissed angrily.

'Fine. No talky nicely, no boxy-woxy.'

Hiss.

'That's better. Release everyone from your mental control. That's mean and unnecessary.'

Instantaneously Michael, the Rivas twins and Chief Hughes staggered and started talking at once, asking what was going on, where they were, how they had come to be... and then they all yelled 'Snakes!' rather pointlessly.

'Shut up!' the Doctor ordered.

They did.

'Glad to have you all back,' he then said a bit more kindly. 'Everyone okay?'

'I feel sick,' said Michael.

'To be expected,' the Doctor said. 'You'll be fine in the morning.'

Commander Cann pushed her way through the protective gang and joined the Doctor and Sam by the Leader Snake.

'Look, sorry, but I demand to know what is going on on my base, Doctor.'

'I don't think it's really your base, Commander.'

'Okay, World State's base.'

'Not what I meant. They see this as *their* base. Been here longer than World State. Longer than UNIT and the base being built to be honest. How many millions of years have you waited?'

The Leader Snake hissed.

'That long? Wow.'

The Doctor took out his Sonic Screwdriver. He aimed it at the large widescreen monitor on the laboratory wall, the one they'd seen Michael and Chief Hughes's voice waveforms on earlier. The screen lit up with a whine. 'Just tuning this into your records, Commander, won't be a sec.'

The holographic solar system appeared upon it.

'That's what we saw earlier,' Michael said.

'Yeah, with that mysterious planet,' Hsui added.

'Which broke up about seventy million years ago,' the Doctor said. 'Sending huge chunks of itself swimming across the solar system, becoming various satellites, moons and asteroids. All that remained of a planet teeming with life. One day it was there, the next – pop – and its gone.'

'You mean this moon is all that remains of it?' asked Sam.

'Possibly. Or maybe the snakes just hitched a lift on your moon a lot earlier, as it was drifting through space. Either way, they've been here a very long time.'

'And now all they want to do is get home?' asked Sam. 'Can we help them?'

'Scary Space Snakes?' the Doctor said to him.

Sam looked at the snakes. 'Not so scary really. Just… a little sad.'

'I like you, Sam, I really do,' said the Doctor. 'Commander Cann, this lad has a good attitude about alien species. You should take him on staff.'

'He's only fourteen,' she said.

'Oh. Oh right. Well then, in a few years. He'll

be an asset.' The Doctor turned back to the Leader Snake. 'But sorry, it's bad news for you guys. Your home is gone. Has been for millions and millions of years.'

The Leader Snake said nothing but Sam realised he and the others were all looking towards the computer screen, staring at the image on it.

The Doctor zapped it again, and the image changed to a contemporary view of the solar system. 'That's how it is now.'

Hiss.

'Possibly,' he said. 'But it would be a dangerous journey. You might be better off staying local, where you know you can survive. It would be a waste to get out there and discover no one else survived. Better to be the last of your people and live, than die out there on a fruitless search for others who may be long dead.'

Hiss.

'Because… because I've never encountered any of them. Anywhere. And I know this system pretty well. I'm not saying it's impossible, but I wouldn't recommend it.'

Hiss.

'Well you just have to negotiate with the lovely Commander here. She's very nice really.'

'Negotiate?' asked Commander Cann. 'I can't speak snake!'

'Perspective, Commander! Communication is a lost art with humans. Learn. Share this Moon, this Moonbase with your neighbours.' The Doctor looked at the Leader Snake. 'Give her a few minutes to digest this.'

'World State's insurance won't cover all this!' Joe Rivas suddenly yelled. 'Alien snakes and stuff!'

Everyone turned to look at him, including his sister, in shock.

'Perspective,' the Doctor said again, shaking his head.

Jo Rivas led her brother to a seat and sat him down.

'I have to know,' the Doctor said, 'how much World State knew about the snakes. Did they expect this? Were you sent here to observe this?'

'We were sent here to make sure the stupid kids didn't get sucked out of an airlock and show them where their stupid murals were going to be painted,' Joe Rivas spat angrily. 'Just 'cos we work for the world's biggest multinational corporation, stop assuming we are the enemy. We didn't ask to be taken over by snakes.'

The Doctor looked at them both, but clearly decided to believe him. Finally he put the red toolbox down on the floor beside the snakes, who immediately surrounded it.

'Don't. Touch.' The Doctor barked. 'You have attacked this Moonbase, hurt the crew, siphoned off power that, left unchecked could have been dangerous to the humans. So before we get into this, we need to work out a plan.'

'I want to know who this Lukas Minski is, and what his connection to the snakes is,' said Chief Christoffel. 'You know, as Security Chief. Sort of thing I ought to know. Isn't it?'

The Doctor smiled. 'Let me tell you what I reckon. Lukas faked his death, his disappearance, because of whatever he put inside this toolbox. He didn't want UNIT getting their hands on it again. He was very brave to do what he did. Lukas worked in a UNIT museum, dealing with things that made him sad because they were often stolen.'

Hissss.

The doctor sighed and looked at the Leader Snake. 'Well, okay, if you know the story smartypants, why not tell it yourself instead of leaving me to work it all out? Brilliantly, I have to say. I'm on the right track, aren't I?'

Hissss.

'Oh right, well there you are then!' He turned to the others. 'Solved.'

'Doctor?' said Commander Cann slowly.

'What now?'

'We don't understand snake?'

'Ah yes, right. Got you. Okay, very simple – UNIT steal alien stuff. Providing it's not weaponry, they put it in a museum, probably utterly unaware of what it is. Enter Lukas Minski, not a rich man, not terribly honest – he nicks something. Gets fired, ends up working up here on the Moon, far away from the authorities on Earth. Meets the snakes – they're drawn to him because he's been in contact with something they have been looking for... for, well, a few thousand, possibly million years – my snake translation is a bit rusty, but I'm plumping for millions. Lukas talks to the snakes –'

'How?' asked Hsui.

'As I said, been in contact with something of theirs. Quick bite on the hand and bingo, instant communication between the two minds – Leader Snake here, Lukas Minski there.'

The Doctor tapped a code in and the box opened.

'How did you know the code?' Commander Cann asked suspiciously.

Sam knew the answer. 'Because the Doctor watched Lukas access it ten years ago.'

As many people as possible clustered round the box, making sure they didn't tread on any snakes.

'A gold egg?' said Christoffel.

The Doctor nodded. 'A golden egg. Yes. A.

Golden. Egg.'

He looked around but no one seemed to understand

And then Sam did. 'Snakes,' he said. 'Snakes hatch from eggs.'

The Doctor beamed. 'That's not a weapon or even a looted work of art. That's the egg of a snake queen – or something similar anyway, could be a king – but that's what that is. Give it to the snakes and everyone can go home.'

'So Lukas made a deal with them,' Sam said slowly, piecing it together. 'He would get them their egg back.'

The Doctor nodded. 'So he went to Earth secretly, got it back eventually – I doubt doing that was entirely above the law – and brought it to the Moon, but the snakes were gone by then. Hiding. World State had moved in, all that change, so they went to ground. Literally. So Lukas hid it in the one place no one was working on, no one was redesigning. HEART.'

Sam looked at the way the snakes were staring

at the egg, mesmerised.

'They just want to go home to a planet they know is gone. How sad.'

'Doctor, you suggested they stay here, yeah?' asked Commander Cann.

Hisss.

'They think you'll kill them,' the Doctor replied.

Commander Cann turned to the Leader Snakes. 'Not going to happen. Ever. Whatever has happened in the past, whatever mistakes were made by the removal of your egg, I apologise on behalf of, well, everyone. This is as much your home as ours. Hell, it's more yours and you surely can make use of the ninety percent we haven't built a Moonbase on. Please, stay. It would be so good to live and work together and learn about one another.'

'Are you sure?' the Doctor said.

'Absolutely,' said the Commander. 'Why, aren't you?'

The Doctor laughed, 'No, no I'm just delighted to hear you say that.'

He passed the egg to the snakes who hissed delightedly.

'Yes,' the Doctor said. 'Look after it better this time and when it's ready to hatch, let the humans know. It'll be a great moment for both your species.'

'Is the egg... okay?' asked Sam. 'I mean, it's been in a toolbox for ten years.'

'It's been an egg on the Moon for a few million years before that, I'm pretty sure it's designed to cope.'

'When is it due to hatch?' Hughes asked.

The Doctor shrugged. 'Probably not in any of your lifetimes.' He looked at Sam. 'Well, maybe yours.'

Joe and Jo Rivas moved to Aaron. 'Did you film all this?' they asked quietly. 'This is going to be huge! You were attacked by the Space Snakes. You'll be a superstar. Give World State that footage and you'll be a star! You could end up the biggest star on the planet!'

Aaron took the camera off his cap and pressed a small switch. The bluetooth connection. 'Actually,

I've erased everything that's been shot so far this trip,' he said quietly. 'No snakes, no attacks, no egg. Nothing. Tomorrow, we can start again, with the guys here and their murals and everything.'

'Are you mad?' Joe Rivas exploded. 'The snake footage is worth ten times some stupid pictures drawn by kids.' He turned to Sam. 'No offence.'

'Lots taken, actually,' said Sam.

Jo Rivas was slightly less hysterical than her brother. 'No back-ups, Aaron?'

'All erased. You're too late,' said Aaron, smiling. 'Can you imagine what would happen if World State knew about the Space Snakes? They'd be up here, dissecting them or something. The snakes should stay the Moon's secret. That's why I've erased it all.'

Joe Rivas shrugged. 'So? We'll tell them what went on. They'll be up here to investigate in days.'

Aaron shrugged. 'But with no footage to back up your claims, why would they believe you?'

'Because everyone here has seen them!' Joe Rivas turned to the Moonbase Laika staff. 'You all work for World State, it's your job to tell them about the Space Snakes.'

'What Space Snakes?' asked Commander Cann. 'Anyone know anything about any Space Snakes?'

'Sounds like a mad old story to me,' said Llewellyn Hughes.

'No idea what Mr Rivas is talking about,' said Godfried Christoffel.

'Just as well,' the Doctor said. 'Look.'

All but one of the snakes had gone. Slithered silently away, carrying the egg, their heritage.

The Leader Snake was still there, swaying slightly as it seemed to weigh up its options.

Hisss.

It slithered away into the ventilation system before anyone could move.

'They'll be in touch,' the Doctor said simply. 'Don't let them down.' He smiled at Commander Cann. 'Don't let *me* down.'

CHAPTER 16
ALIVE AND KICKING

Sam was at home, on Earth, in his back garden. His parents were shopping and he was sat in the sunshine, reading a book. About snakes.

The *BPXtra* shows had gone out. Moonbase Laika was decorated with all the murals, Aaron Relevy had struck a deal to regularly do shows from the Moon about life up there, with Hsui as a co-host and, Sam reckoned, a bit more. Caitlin, Michael and especially Savannah had all stayed in touch with him. Four friends for life.

He wondered if he'd ever see the Doctor again.

As if in answer, the doorbell rang and he went to answer it.

The Doctor was there, grinning. 'Hullo, Sam, glad I didn't miss you. Last time I knocked, you'd got an engineering degree, married Savannah, moved to Switzerland and this place was occupied by a strange old lady with twelve cats.' He stopped. 'Probably shouldn't have told you that – future's a funny old thing. Anyway, glad you're still here and still fourteen years old. Got someone who wants to say hullo.'

He moved aside and Sam could see an old man standing by the gate.

It was the same old man he'd met before, back at the *BPXtra* studios, although better dressed now. He was even wearing a bow tie. Clearly he'd been out shopping with the Doctor.

They shook hands and Lukas Minski started to thank Sam for everything he'd done to get the egg back to the snakes. 'You were magnificent according to the Doctor. Very brave.'

The Doctor smiled. 'We're heading back to Russia tomorrow – his family is so excited that they are going to be reunited. And I pulled a few strings with UNIT to clear his name.'

'After so many years, they thought I was dead. Now I can see them again. My Annika will be all grown up – I have missed so much of her life...'

'Anyway, we just wanted to say bye and thank you,' the Doctor said.

'Hang on,' said Sam. 'When we were leaving Moonbase Laika, Commander Cann gave me something, in case we ever met again Mr Minski.'

Sam rushed up to his bedroom, pulled out a box from under his bed and headed back down again. He passed it over.

'She said you might want it.'

Frowning, Lukas opened the box.

It was a home-made moon buggy, next to a card in Lukas's handwriting.

To my beloved daughter annika. Happy tenth birthday.

'Thank you,' Lukas said quietly. 'Better late than never,' he said, and gave Sam a huge hug. 'For everything.'

Lukas Minski walked back down the path, holding the buggy tightly.

The Doctor shook Sam's hand. 'Goodbye for now. I look forward to meeting you again, in Switzerland. Something to do with solving the Oil Apocalypse, I seem to recall. We make a great team. Or did. Or will. Whatever.'

And he was gone.

But Sam knew that it wouldn't be the last time he saw the Doctor.

Because life was good like that.

THE END

DOCTOR WHO

The journey through time and space never ends...
For more exciting adventures, look out for

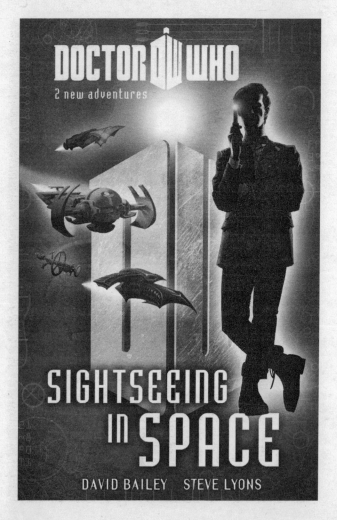

DOCTOR DW WHO

The journey through time and space never ends...
For more exciting adventures, look out for

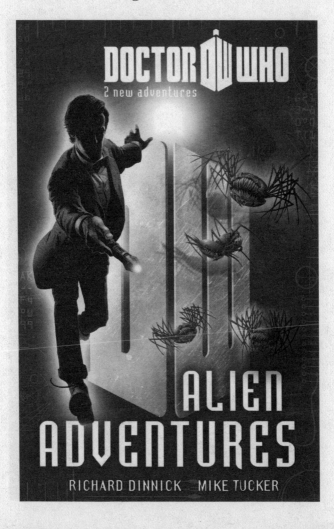

DOCTOR WHO

The journey through time and space never ends...
For more exciting adventures, look out for